Sunbathing in Siberia

ELIZABETH LEWIS

DIVA

All characters in this novel are fictitious and any resemblance
to real persons, living or dead, is purely coincidental.

First published 2003 by Diva Books,
an imprint of Millivres Prowler Limited, part of the Millivres Prowler Group,
Unit M, Spectrum House, 32-34 Gordon House Road, London NW5 1LP UK

www.divamag.co.uk

A catalogue record for this book is available from the British Library

ISBN 1-873741-82-0

Printed and bound in Finland by WS Bookwell

Distributed in the UK and Europe by Airlift Book Company,
8 The Arena, Mollison Avenue,
Enfield, Middlesex EN3 7NJ
Telephone: 020 8804 0400

Distributed in North America by Consortium,
1045 Westgate Drive, St Paul, MN 55114-1065
Telephone: 1 800 283 3572

Distributed in Australia by Bulldog Books,
PO Box 300, Beaconsfield, NSW 2014

Acknowledgements

Many thanks to Kathleen Bryson, Sue Harper and Helen Sandler from Diva Books for their help, advice and encouragement.

'Trying to be his lover was like sunbathing in Siberia'

Graeme Aitken, *Vanity Fierce*

Part One

One

The best and the worst thing about humanity is surely our unparalleled ability to adapt to circumstance.

In we stagger, my partner and I, crushed under the weight of a greenish-blue sofa-bed. We scoured all of West London for it today, with increasing desperation. Jay's parents are coming to stay and we live in a one-bedroom flat. Aargh. They don't know we're a couple. Double Aargh! And Jay, whatever she says when drunk, has no intention of telling them, now or – probably – ever. Triple Aargh! Quadruple Aargh. Enough Aargh to last a lifetime. But at this stage it doesn't even occur to me to protest. Sadly, I seem to have adapted perfectly to life in the closet.

These days, 'the closet' is a ground-floor flat in Baron's Court, West Kensington. Our friends Ross and Robbie, being rich, have the rest of the house. It's one of those large, mansion-style white things, and our flat is gorgeous, sunlit and homey, but so small that the little white hall runs parallel to all the rooms. Said hall is taken up with a long ledge, on which sit some plants (Jay's babies) and assorted odds and ends. Framed pictures of cats and boats and the odd postcard that we both like run along the wall, battling with the babies to be seen.

If said babies *were* human, they'd be terrified right now as we rock unsteadily past them, threatening decapitation and amputation with every tilt of this bed-shaped closet.

'Be careful!' she snaps as we thud into the ledge yet again, scaring a quivering begonia. Typical Jay: *we* make a mistake and *I* get blamed for it.

Ah, but she's lovely, my love. Short, plump, dark hair, may not sound like Sharon Stone but she's so cute, like a little bear. And her nose turns up, and her mouth is adorable and soft, and she – being obsessive about cleaning everything from the flat to herself – always smells deliciously fresh and perfumed.

I'm shorter – 5'2 to her 5'4 – a year younger than her 30 and, after six years, still wildly in love with her. Sometimes, though, she just pisses me off to the point where I could hit her.

'I am being careful!' I hiss back and dump the fucking thing unceremoniously on the floor: '*There*! Are you happy now?'

Jay, damn her eyes, puts her end down carefully. 'Not really, no,' she purrs. She's also got a really nice voice, gravelly, with a hint of Irish. If a bear could talk, it would talk like Jay. Panting, we both look at the sofa-bed.

'D'you think it looks as though it's been here as long as we have?' she asks.

I gaze at it. It's positively squatting there. It could have been dropped off by aliens. It's also twice the size of our blue and white one, and doesn't exactly look happy to be here; clearly it was meant for better things. One thing it doesn't seem is familiar.

'No.'

We've been in this flat almost six months now. We've been living together for over four years, all in all. Not that we ever call it living together. We call it 'sharing a flat'. And it certainly hasn't been without incident. Half a year with us and this sofa would look like it had been through Beirut.

'Well, my parents think it's been your bed for the past six months –'

'Right!'

I jump onto it and leap around a bit. Jay is horrified and hisses, 'Stop that!' in her most administrative voice.

'I'm ju-husst,' I wheeze, 'ma-*ha*king it look like it's been here as lo-ho-ng a-has we haave...'

'No! Now help me get the little truckle bed in.' And off she stomps, into the hall.

The Little Truckle Bed. One of the reasons it took us so damn long to get the sofa was that we – for 'we' read Jay – needed one with this truckle bed thing.

'Oh good, the little truckle bed,' I mince, as we stagger in with it, 'essential furnishing for every closet', and then I drop the damn thing on my foot.

'*Ow!*'

Jay, now the happiest she's been all day, is suitably sympathetic. 'Serves you right. So,' she huffs, pushing it under the Alien, 'it just fits under the bed like *that* –'

'Owww!' I moan now, to get attention back to my wound. It doesn't work.

'Right!' says Jay briskly, 'you and I'll be sleeping in here –' she waves her arm about the sitting-room, and just guess who's going to get the truckle bed, 'and remember, if they ask, this –' she slaps the sofa thing, and we finish in unison, 'was always your bed.'

'I *know*,' I hiss.

Jay starts to pat the sofa-bed perfectly into place. 'Just checking... and that we wanted a two-bedroom flat, but couldn't afford it, and that you wanted the sitting-room because the bedroom was too noisy for you –'

'Fat chance...' I mutter. Jay likes her love-making silent.

She over-rides me. 'Because it looks over a main road.' She pauses to re-align the bed. 'And remember, while they're here, no touching each other, no loving looks, and on *no account* talk about anything gay or lesbian –'

'Are you *sure* that you're going to be telling them about us sometime soon?'

Jay sits on the sofa – the actual sofa, not this new schizophrenic one – and looks in the mirror to smooth her (short) hair down.

'Yes,' she concurs, 'but I'll choose the moment. I don't want them to –' here her voice muffles as she bends down to retie her sensible shoes '– discover it for themselves,' and up she sits. She shoots her cuffs back to look at her large steel watch and stamps off.

'No-o-o,' I say to the empty air, 'the shock would kill them.'

Oh fuck. They're coming tomorrow.

Two

I'd tottered awake, that first morning, with a hang-over and vague sense that something had happened last night, that I'd inched out onto a ledge far above ground level. Then I saw Jay and remembered.

It had been late; our flatmate had long since gone to bed. Jay and I stayed in her room, drinking. I was half-way through a litre bottle of vodka, she was on her eighth Guinness. I remembered the room swinging around me; I remembered Jay saying quietly, 'I really like you.'

'I really like you, too,' I'd slurred back, thinking, 'How cute.'

'No, I mean *really* like... fancy.'

She'd looked down, vulnerable. Ridiculously, what went whirling through my head was a passage from an astrology book I'd been reading earlier: 'Libra, Pisces, Gemini and Aquarius are the four signs most likely to fall in love with members of their own sex... or to experiment.' Jay's an Aquarian. It made me feel terribly tender towards her, this suggestion that she might be in the grip of the Cosmos.

'Oh, *darling,*' I said and lunged forward to hug her, and then we were kissing. Then – I was very drunk – blackness started to appear round the edges of the room. More and more came, until all that was left was a little diamond of light, which got thinner and thinner as the darkness encroached on it, until it was just a sliver, then nothing.

Bits and pieces of that night eventually came back to me – Jay and I kissing, lying down together, a memory of time passing, but the main part of it will forever remain a blur.

Something like this was bound to happen. Jay and I had been becoming closer and closer. I'd been happier than ever before. She'd also got under my skin more than anyone else, annoyed me more than anyone else. I'd been talking about her to anyone who'd listen. If she'd been a man, someone would have pointed out the obvious. As it was, people just looked at me a bit strangely then changed the subject.

We were in Inverness, with Jay's friend Josie. They both worked in one of the large hotels there, Josie as a receptionist, Jay as administrator. They'd known each other for about two years and hit it off really well, so, when they got sick of the staff quarters, they had got a place together. Then they'd run out of money and decided to take in a lodger. I'd been posted to the Highlands for the summer to cover someone's maternity leave in a branch of the travel agency I worked for. It was a temporary promotion, then I'd be going back to London. I'd seen their ad in the *Inverness Courier*, applied, and moved in the next day. That was two months since and I'd never had so much fun. And then spring came and Inverness was beautiful, and the air, which I'd thought was going to kill me when I arrived, turned balmy, and was so pure that every breath I took seemed to cleanse me.

'Yeah...' Josie had muttered when I said that to her, 'easy to say that when you're only up for the summer. I'd love to live in London.'

'Well, then, go for it,' I replied. 'Come down. You'll get a job easily, stay with me...' to which she shook her head doubtfully and said, 'Maybe one day...'

She belonged there. She was lovely – tall, slim, blonde hair, deep, raspy voice – and had a keen interest in the lads, who reciprocated gleefully. There was always one or another hanging round the flat hopefully.

All the people dropping in gave the place the air of a constant party. I loved it. Jay and I, shorter and fatter than Josie, didn't attract men the way she did (nor did we seem to want to) but we had a lot of fun listening to her conquests, giggling, messing about, just the three of us. I hadn't been sober for a night since I arrived and my alcohol tolerance had increased dramatically. I'd never drunk half a litre of vodka before, though.

I levered myself up, looked at Jay. She was lying under the bedclothes, the mound of her body curled around mine. 'Tangled like puppies,' I thought, glowing. Just then her alarm rasped. She jumped, remembered, looked around. It was a supremely awkward moment. Neither of us had ever done anything like it before. Each was wondering if the other was repelled.

I had only a bra and knickers on; she was wearing a nightshirt. I saw the pink of it as she raised her arm above the duvet.

'Hi...' I croaked, and she smiled at me, and I was bathed in warmth. She wanted me, and I – I was already in love.

'I've got to go to work,' she whispered. 'Will I see you this evening?' From the way she asked it, I knew she was serious too.

I nodded, smiling from ear to ear: 'Here? About six?'

'Fine.'

I got up, feeling ridiculously self-conscious, and looked for my clothes. Clutching them to me, I slithered to the door, checked the corridor, turned to smile goodbye at Jay. Time stopped on that moment for me, like a painting or a photo, and I remember her curled there under the duvet. I remember her black hair shining and tousled on top of her head; I remember the flimsy drawn curtains, sun streaming in from behind them so that she lay in a pool of light. I remember how she was raised slightly on one shoulder, the glimpse of pink that was her nightshirt, before the green duvet drowned it. And I remember... will always remember, when all else has been forgotten, how she smiled at me.

I was still slightly drunk. I went back to my room, lay down, tried to sleep, couldn't. I was so excited. I was in love.

It was my day off. Later, when a shop-girl pressed my change into my hand, smiling, I smiled back, then felt (thrilling to it) like a wolf in sheep's clothing. I was now predator. I, as much as any man, loved women.

It felt that something that had been rough and difficult, like a jagged seam, had knit itself together; lay smooth before me. *This* was my path. It wasn't a shock. I'd gone out with men before but, whenever one of them tried to kiss me, I'd recoiled in disgust and anger at their presuming to think I could want them. Exactly the reaction a straight man would have, I thought, and skipped a little.

I'd walked back in a daze. Jay. Juliette. Juliette Barrie. Short, cute, beautiful brown eyes, tiny nose, and her mouth... It was her mouth I dwelt on at the start of 'us', on the line of it, the softness, the firmness of it. Not over-fleshy, but not too thin, a perfect size, and tilted up a little. Almost red, but not quite, deeper than pink, there isn't a word for the colour. My mind's eye saw it perfectly. I'd wanted to see it in reality again.

She came home at five-thirty; came to my room. We looked

shyly at each other. I was joyful, my heart singing, 'She's the one.' Attraction flared between us again. We walked slowly toward each other in exquisite mutual knowledge and anticipation. My arms went round her, and we kissed.

She had the most beautiful body; cream and curved, mysterious. I lay behind, curved into her, one hand trailing over her stomach, touching her breasts, my fingers making her nipples harden. And I needed to have her again, to possess. To take her independence and make it mine.

I kissed her neck, breathed her scent, sought her lips again. Heat and gentleness and passion moved in me as one. I shifted, so I was looking down on her, bent my head to her breasts, to suckle and caress, feel her arch against me. I wanted to have every part of her at once, to give and possess at the same time. My hand caressed its way down her stomach, felt the excitement of her pubic hair, slid at last into the wetness, into the mysteries of her. She sighed, moved, and the rest of the world disappeared as I stroked and entered her; as the rhythm began.

Afterwards, we lay, wet and entwined. My head was on her breast. I heard her heartbeat, smiled up at her, told her.

'What does it sound like?'

Like lovers everywhere, I described it.

'That's nice,' she smiled sleepily.

We dozed, woke to hear Josie arrive, giggled helplessly when she called, 'Anybody home?'

And then we were caught up in the warm, rose-scented whirlwind of sex again.

We stayed in my bed. Moonlight replaced the sun. Intimacy deepened. The feel of her body, her smell, the way she moved, were being etched on my mind and in my senses. I felt that shift inside that is the true consummation, without which the questing penetration of sex stays forever frustrated, unable to reach the deeps.

It felt as if I was making space for her inside my very heart, that my bloodstream was clotting together there to make a foundation, a placenta for the invisible cord that linked us. The cord that would, from this night on, forever tug on my heart, would send pain through my bloodstream, when I was not with her. Like all who love for the first time, I saw only the driving-force of the joining, and so held nothing back. From her rapt look, intent on me, I guessed she was feeling the same: how could I have felt this if she were not opening to me also?

I smiled at her. It was all so exquisitely new. I kissed her lips again, unable to help myself. They curved into a smile under me, opened slightly, and our tongues touched, curled gently together.

Sated, we knew this was just a kiss, a tacit agreement of our connection.

I had to kiss my way down her throat, to nuzzle into her

breasts, to touch her everywhere again until she squirmed away, laughing, protesting that it was too soon.

'Mmmm... I know.' Gently, I ran my hand down the curve of her belly till it was under her back.

She turned into me. My arm slipped down, hers went round me. As close as we could be, we sighed in contentment.

The night passed in magic.

'Did you always know?' I asked, at one point.

'Know what?'

'That you liked women?'

'I think so.'

'I didn't. No idea, until –'

'Until I seduced you.'

'I don't remember –'

Her laugh rippled round me. 'I've never been that drunk before... I'd never have asked you if I hadn't been.'

'Thanks!' I chuckled with the confidence of the loved.

'You know what I mean.'

'Yes.'

I kissed her again, as the night touched us gently, drew back, smiled. The length of our naked bodies pressed against each other. I touched her face softly, amazed at the intimacy.

'Were you confident that I'd say yes?'

'I didn't know what you'd do.' Her voice was amused at her own daring.

'What if I'd screamed and said no, and that I'd tell everyone?'

'I knew you wouldn't do that.'

I smiled, caressed. The night went on. Later: 'When did you first want to ask me?'

'I don't know... for some time now.'

I stretched luxuriously. 'I had no idea.'

'I thought you did.'

'Nope... complete shock.'

'Nice shock?'

I reared up. Propped on an elbow, I looked down at her, shivered with the exquisite sense of merging, this metamorphosis of stranger to part of me. My very molecules were dancing with her dizzying entrance... and vice-versa.

'Amazing...' Fiercely, I bent, kissed her, felt the rush as particles came rushing out of our shared bloodstream to dance together, blending and mating until there was no 'Jay' or 'Miranda', only a synthesis of the two of us – that strange third form destined to leap into being whenever we are together, until one of us kills it by withdrawing.

Finally, we slept, went to work exhausted when her alarm rang. Work seemed unreal. All I thought about was Jay's body, the triumph I felt when she first moved and bucked under me, losing control as orgasm came, the sight of her, the sound of her sex-tossed sighs, ending with that small exhalation of relief and satisfaction. The scent of her, which was still on my fingers, a beautiful, ghostly memory.

When colleagues spoke to me or smiled at me, when work was hard, I inhaled her, and smiled. I felt outlawed by my secret, thought, wondering, 'Last night, I made a woman come!'

I left work early, pleading an appointment, arrived back at four-thirty to find her already there. We went to my room and she looked at me fiercely, as though I was something she had hungered for, wanted to devour. I shivered, knowing that I was going to be opened again, felt the almost scared thrill of the desired, knew I was looking at her in the same way.

We lay down on my bed and kissed. The day blended away, as dreams do. *This* was reality.

That was a golden summer. The weather was glorious, the scenery celestially beautiful: the River Ness, with the castle on the hill beyond it, purple heather carpeting the slopes below. Trees rustled in the fresh summer winds, waving their branches to underscore the sky. The air was so pure that there was no room for illusion, spreading over the panorama, giving the colours transparency, as though they were glazed and kept under glass.

The Highland sky stretched forever, containing us all, curving round, making the ground dip under our feet with its vastness, the mountains stretching through the purple clouds of sunset to reach it.

The colours... the freshest of greens in the branches and ferns flanked the rushing grey and silver river, sometimes mismatched by the light-blue sky roofing them, which changed hue from the cool grey of dawn to the scarlet and gold of the spreading sunset. Then, before the first stars appeared, it changed to a blue I'd never seen anywhere else, bringing stillness for the day as it died.

All these draped the 'third person', so that when I think of the start of 'us', I see the shimmering colours of that summer. They were the perfect cloth on which to spread our love affair. I saw them all, sunrise to sunset, because I wasn't sleeping. I wasn't eating either. I lost a stone and a half, and, for the first time, felt really pretty. Jay and I glowed.

We didn't tell Josie about 'us' until four years later. 'You mean, that whole summer, you were –?'

We nodded sheepishly, grinning.

'You buggers! I didn't have a clue! Not a bloody clue...! And are you still –?'

We nodded again.

'Stone me! Well, good for you!'

Josie is one of the truly generous of this world, in that there is no prejudice in her. She was already a single parent, her adventures with men having led her inevitably to that point, and her babies are lucky. I can picture her years later, her slender body thickened slightly, her highlighted hair silvering, and she will still be glamorous, still laughing her throaty laugh, and all the neighbourhood kids will come to her for help and advice. Her sons will see in her the very essence of womanhood, and they'll be right.

But we didn't tell her. We didn't tell anyone. Secrecy intensified everything, but it was a light-hearted secrecy, with none of the angst that was to come later. Jay's parents, visiting her brother in Canada for that year, were completely out of the picture, with not even a shadow of their rabid anti-gay sentiments remaining to haunt us.

The time of my leaving came upon us slowly. Lying on my bed, we'd discussed it a lot, but never with the realisation that it was going to happen.

'Maybe Elaine won't want to come back to work,' I'd said hopefully.

'What are you going to do if she does?'

'I'll ask if they'll keep me on in some capacity.'

'Weren't you saying earlier that they're not very impressed with you?'

'Yes, but I'll say I'll improve; say I was – distracted –' I bit her ear gently.

It was true, my performance at work was abysmal. Thanks to the wonder of love, I'd been day-dreaming half the time I was at work, which wasn't very often. I'd called in sick five times, had one dentist's appointment, taken every bank holiday. I was also dog-tired. There had been better things to do in life than sleep.

Jay sat up, looked at me seriously. 'Could you stay up here permanently?'

I stared back at her, she who was now so familiar. The thought of leaving her was... unimaginable.

'Of course I could. I'm going to. Something'll come up.'

'Start looking for jobs, just in case. I'll get the *Courier*.'

But I couldn't find anything. Bloody Elaine proved unnaturally eager to leave her baby and, with insincere expressions of regret from everybody, I was out.

'Come and visit me soon,' I begged, at the airport.

'Of course I will.' Jay looked as sick as I felt. 'Phone me when you get there.'

'I will.'

'Last call for London Flight BR2990. Last call for –'

Jay stepped forward and hugged me, enveloping me in safe and blessed blackness.

'I love you,' she whispered fiercely. We stayed like that for a minute, then she pulled away, kissed me on the lips, and said, 'You'd better go.'

The cord tugged painfully between us as I walked toward the boarding area, unable to believe this was happening. I looked round, saw her standing forlorn, as bereft as I was. I waved, blew a kiss, saw her return it, and then I had to turn, get on that bloody aeroplane.

Then I lived for her calls and letters and the odd weekend together, when the colours glowed vivid again.

Six months later, she phoned to say she'd got that job in London and would be down in a month. We moved in together the month after that.

I was so happy.

Three

Then her parents returned from Canada. A week later she started to hit me.

Soon it seemed amazing that there had been a time when I had been utterly open before her. I still loved her; it was still magical, but the pain had begun. Less and less often did I feel absolute togetherness with her, and such times, instead of being the norm, became the reason I put up with the loneliness.

And that golden summer changed in my memory, as if a sliver of enchanted steel had been put in it, turning the fresh, rooted greens and blues to the lurid, sliding, sickened colours of Now. Grown used to the necessity of barriers, I would look back and think, no, it couldn't have been like *that*, there was never a time I trusted her so completely, even then, I must have known...

Four

I jolt awake at eight o'clock on the Saturday morning before the visit because the space beside me is empty. I look blearily around and the deserted bedroom comes fully into focus. I *hate* it when she does this. She's so fucking independent. She'll be off somewhere, in her shell, withdrawn. The stress of the visit has started already. Oh well, so what? If she can't wake me up and share it with me, sod *her*. I roll over and try to go back to sleep. And give up. I want us to be together. I hate the *space* of Jay in a bad mood. I get up, shove on my dressing-gown (navy-blue towelling with yellow squiggles, past its best, Jay hates it) and pad into the sitting-room. There she is, sitting on the couch in her dressing-gown (light blue with tiny white flowers all over it. A present from her sister Sinead, it's far too femme for her, but she wears it religiously), a notepad and pen beside her, staring blankly into space.

The curtains are still drawn and a yellow light suffuses the room. It's quite cosy, makes it feel as if we're hiding. I try not to look at the glowering green sofa-bed. I smile at Jay. She stares back, looks away.

'Good morning.'

Jay ignores me. We're off.

'Good *morning*!' I say pointedly, and this time she grunts.

'Do you know what time it is?' I ask lightly.

There is a pause. I crack first.

'It's eight o'clock!' Still nothing. 'Why are we up at eight on a Saturday morning?' Pause. 'Jay!!' Pause. 'Will you stop being so bloody rude and *talk* to me?'

'I'm OK,' she finally says coolly, just as my nerve is at breaking point, 'you go back to bed.'

'Right,' I snap, rebuffed yet again, 'I will.'

I turn to go, then stop. Maybe all is not lost. As seductively as I can, I murmur, 'Come with me?'

'No, I've got too much to do.'

'Like *what*?'

She looks at me as if I've gone mad. 'Like what? My *parents* are coming today –'

'Are they?' I bellow, 'Are they really? You should have *said something...*'

She stares at me again, with contempt, then says, 'I think you should go back to bed.'

'Oh, so do I!' I stamp out. Two minutes later I'm back. I sit beside the gorgon and put my arm around her shoulder. 'Come on, what's up? Tell me.'

Another silence. How does she do it?

'*Tell* me...'

Another small eternity goes by. I've actually started to count the seconds. They say you should let at least ten go by. That's the length of time it can take. Whoever said that didn't know Jay. Instead of counting seconds, you can count hours. I'm seriously considering bringing a book.

Eventually she stirs, and says tiredly, 'Oh, just so much to do –' and I tut.

She stops.

'Sorry, go on.' Please go on. Mentally, I slap-slap my wrist.

'That's it, really... And, oh, I dunno, just – I don't know – my parents coming, the whole pressure of it. You know what they're like... I just woke up in a downer this morning.'

I put my other arm around her and pull her into a hug. As though I can infuse her with hope, with love for me, I breathe into her. My strength for the both of us.

'Silly person,' I croon, 'silly person. It's going to be fine. They love you. That's not going to change, ever...'

'I wish I was as sure of that as you,' Jay says, half wryly, half painfully, well aware of the horrendously awful fate that could await her. I take a deep breath.

'It isn't going to change,' I blunder, 'but, say it did – I really don't think it would, but just imagine – wouldn't it be better to find out now and get over it, rather than spend the next twenty years in that *miserable* closet and never know if they would've accepted you? Just think what a relief it would be if they knew – none of this stress of "Do they/don't they know? Ohmygod, I think they suspect, quick, *do* something." Think how nice it'll be to be yourself.'

I stop, panting for breath.

'Yes' says Jay reasonably, 'you're right; I know you're right.' My heart skips a little. Progress. I don't completely have her yet; she keeps too much distance between us. 'It's just,' she continues, 'that, if they reject me, I won't be able to deal with it.'

'Yes, you will, and you'll have me to help you...'

'Thanks, but if they do reject me, no one'll be able to help.'

I want to strangle her. I stare miserably round the flat instead, and then throw myself into good-patient-lover mode.

'Well, you're not coming out to them this weekend, so *this* had better go,' and down come our two entwined ornamental ladies, 'and this,' concealing the *Penguin Book of Lesbian Short Stories*, 'and definitely *this*,' pushing past the pain barrier, and into a cupboard goes the framed photo of us that I love, one of Jay and me taken in Cambridge, on the bank of the Cam. You can see the river darkly in the background. Jay's wearing a bottle-green coat and a hat and I've got on some white affair, and we're smiling into each other's eyes, very close, lips almost touching.

Something of the spirit of 'us' is captured in that photo; we look as though we belong together.

I sigh, stare at a cat ornament. 'What about that?'

'I think it's safe to leave it.'

'Well, she *is* the only pussy either of us'll be seeing for a while... Right! They'll be here for dinner?'

'Right.'

'So, what're we giving them?' I ask, moving forward into the controlled space of guest-preparation.

It works, though not quite the way I'd imagined.

'OK,' Jay leaps up, galvanised. 'I'll do this part of it – you go and get dressed and then you can go to the shops while I clean in here.'

Uh-*huh*. Well, at least she's back in action. Occasionally, I feel that I would like the odd say in my life, but on the whole it's usually too much trouble and she does end up being right about the practical things. We're not really butch and femme, we're *us*. It's just that Jay is naturally in control, or she's not... well, Jay. And it's easier to go along with her than make up with her afterwards.

'Right you are, sir,' I say now, jokily saluting, grateful she's making an effort, and as I turn to go she murmurs, 'I love you...'

I turn back. 'I love you too... and it'll be fine.' I look at her and feel soft to my bones with love for, and belonging to, her. 'See you in a bit.'

As I am ready to go, she shoves a list into my hand. 'Right. I'll just take you through the list.'

'Jay, I think I can –'

'Now, it's new potatoes, but if they don't have them, then get King Edwards. If they don't have them... but they will have. I've only put "cream" down, but make sure you don't get whipping: we don't have time to stand there doing it. Tuna – make sure it's in brine, not sunflower oil, OK? And don't get... Miranda, are you taking all this in?'

'Yes-s-s...'

'Good!' Here she pats me patronisingly on the back. 'Tomatoes, don't get real ones –'

'What do I get then? Plastic? In case the real ones aren't shiny enough for your parents? Quite right, can't be too careful.'

'Don't get *real* ones,' she over-rides me, 'Get tinned ones. And not ones with garlic and herbs in, just plain.'

And I find this woman sexy!

'Right! All *right*! Now I'm going.'

'No, there's more I've got to tell you –' she wails earnestly, but by this time I'm heading for the door.

'Jay! If you give me one more instruction, you can go and get the bloody things yourself, OK?'

'OK.'

One thing about her, she does know when to stop. I blow her a kiss and head for the door.

'Justmakesureyougetachickenthat'scornfedit'sveryimportant Miranda.'

I was wrong.

'I mean it! If you can't get a corn-fed chicken, don't get one at all!'

Five

I scowl down at what seems like hundreds of frozen chickens, while shoppers stream around me. Occasionally they tut when they have to reach past my unyielding form and stretch out to get to the frozen fowl they want, but I don't care.

I've been here nearly five minutes now. I have hit a snag and, until I resolve it, I can't move forward. I am in a horrible, horrible Dilemma. The problem is that, while half the chickens are beautifully corn-fed and are a glaring yellow to prove it, they are the frozen ones. The other half, while being beautifully unfrozen, have been fed on something else.

This is the sort of thing that, should I make the wrong decision, could drive Jay bananas. Solomon in all his glory couldn't have solved this one. (Note: had Jay been the real mother of that child, when Solomon said he'd tear it in half, she'd have called his bluff.)

Eventually, after a lot of soul-searching, I decide on the corn-fed one, on the basis that I'd probably be safer to follow orders.

But the triumph of getting exactly the right tomatoes, potatoes and cream dims slightly in the shadow of the knowledge that All is Not as Jay Has Ordered. I've been brainwashed.

Still, I have got everything on the list and am feeling a sense of achievement as I hump it all back to the flat.

I should have known better. By the time I've staggered back, laden with six extremely heavy carrier bags, Jay's good mood has evaporated. I find her cleaning the kitchen, spraying huge clouds of Dettox around. I dump the two bags I've brought in and sourly announce, 'There's four more outside.'

Jay sighs heavily and slowly puts down her cloth, like a priest being dragged from his prayers by the demands of the ungodly. I see red.

'Considering I've humped them all the way from the supermarket, it won't kill you to bring four of them in all the way from the *front step*!'

'All *right*!'

She stomps off and I lift the bags onto a (sparkling clean, no bacteria anywhere, we'll probably die from the first germ we encounter outside) counter. It's hard lifting them when I have to lift my very heavy heart along with them. Especially when one of them contains the chicken. I'm unpacking the second one when Jay comes in, four weighty bags dangling from her wrists like bracelets. She takes one look at the chicken and stops dead.

'What,' she says, in a voice like the crack of doom, 'is *that*?'

Clearly, prevarication is useless.

'It's a *chicken,'* and, with forced bravado, I continue the unpacking, although my every muscle is tensed and turning my back on her terrifies me.

I jump at her next comment: 'I specifically told you to get an unfrozen, corn-fed chicken.'

Fear and misery can combine to make rage and I explode now.

'Well, the only corn-fed ones they had were frozen,' I scream. 'I must've stood for about half an hour at that bloody freezer, trying to decide. In the end, I thought, "Get a frozen, corn-fed one, we can always defrost it." I thought that that would be easier than trying to transform the other one.'

We are standing there glaring at each other when Ross comes in.

I adore Ross. He and his partner Robbie have the flat upstairs and they've turned into good friends, of mine if not so much Jay's. They don't really approve of Jay.

Ross is in his mid-thirties, tall, slim, with a thin face that has too many lines on it for his age, elegant in a slightly camp sort of way. Today, he's wearing a cream shirt and trousers, green patterned waistcoat and black shoes that I swear have a greeny tinge about them.

He always wears long-sleeved things, even in the height of summer. When he was eighteen, he came out to his parents, who promptly disowned him. His boyfriend dumped him, and his best friend told him to never speak to him again. If he'd had a dog, Ross jokes bitterly, no doubt it would have attacked him too, turned into Old Yeller after the rabies got it.

After his 'best friend' had told him to fuck off ('frigging shirt-lifter, you disgust me!'), Ross checked into a cheap hotel, bought a packet of razor blades from Boots ('they don't really sell them these days, I had to fucking ask the assistant if they had any... she was very helpful') and slit his wrists.

He was found by the hotel manager, who'd come up to tell him his credit card wasn't working ('not exactly the sort of news to make you want to come back, was it?') and rushed to hospital. His parents didn't come to see him, nor did his ex-best friend. His other friends did, though, along with someone from a young gay men's group, and Ross started his life over again. He only told me all this because one night I got very drunk and very upset over Jay and ended up at their place, sobbing and swearing and declaring that if I had a gun, right then, I'd pull the trigger.

Ross could tell that I meant it and we ended up having intense discussion all night. Robbie eventually went off to bed in a slight huff and next day Jay was only worried in case I'd told him 'personal things' about her. Which I had.

Ross sympathises with Jay's fear of rejection from her parents, but I think he rather despises her for reaching thirty and still being too scared to tell them.

Before Ross, I'd never believed that lesbians and gay men could be friends. Apart from 'the common cause', what do we really have in common? We can have babies together (and boo-sucks to the straights who prophesied childlessness and lonely old age for us all) but in my darker moments, when I've seen too many instances of gay men being nasty to lesbians, I've wondered if they're jealous of us. We do have an easier time of it, and always have done. Or is it just that men are nasty to women generally and the gay community is no different?

The arrival of Ross and Robbie in my life, and gradually a lot of their friends, came as a huge relief. They have the spare keys to our front door and we have theirs. Hence Ross's sudden appearance.

'What *are* you talking about?' he asks now. 'Or is it better I don't know?' Just then he catches sight of the chicken and gasps theatrically, one hand clasped to his bosom. 'Dear God! What is that? And thank heaven it's dead.'

Neither of us laugh and I yell at him, 'It's a chicken, all right, it's a bloody *chicken*! It's a frozen, corn-fed, delicious CHICKEN! Anyway,' I lower my voice, 'it's more alive than Juliette's parents.'

Jay glowers at me. 'At least *my* mother can't crack glass with a smile.'

'Your mother couldn't crack glass with a hammer.'

'That's because my mother's gentle and caring.'

'Yeah...?'

'Oooh, is this going to turn into a full-blown domestic, with china and... chicken flying all over the place? Because, if so, I'll go back upstairs and listen with Robbie from a place of safety.'

'Well, tell her about us, and see how gentle and caring she is then,' I screech.

Jay gives me a look of hatred and stomps out the room. We hear the hat-stand shake, the front door slams. There is a pause.

'Parent trouble?' Ross asks, finally.

'Parent terror,' I sigh. 'They're arriving tonight and she's terrified that they'll find out about us, that somehow something'll slip out and... oh, everything's got to be "perfect" for them, the bigoted old fools,' I say meanly, then immediately remember all the kindnesses they've shown me. 'I didn't mean that. They're very sweet really and I'm fond of them...' I trail off, realising for the umpteenth time just how little I can trust that sweetness.

'But they are bigoted?' asked Ross, going straight to the only thing that really counts.

'Oh, yes. Homosexuality is evil, it's against God's law, it's good for a nice straight laugh and no child of theirs could ever be so unnatural...'

Ross is silent. I suppose that he's remembering his past and my suspicions are confirmed when he looks at his arms, to the places where the scars are hidden, and then says, in a voice rich with understanding, 'Oh, the pain that can cause and the frustration, the feeling of being so... cut off. It must be very hard for her... and for you...'

He is asking me, with great sincerity, if I'd like to talk, and the old sick feeling comes back, the feeling that is me noticing the gap between what a normal, good relationship would be like and the one I've got. The chasm is deep and black and is the measure of the pain and fear I never feel. Because to feel it would mean being lost in the middle of that swirling blackness, where you can see neither up nor down, nor ending...

The chasm is in me and, when I do catch glimpses of it, it feels as if I'm being cut in two by the pain, by the knowledge of how little Jay really loves me.

I gasp, dizzy with it, then say brightly, 'No, it's OK most of the time.'

(There is a silence, during which we both remember the night I staggered upstairs, crying hysterically over and over again, 'She doesn't love me at all, she never has, and oh, it hurts, it hurts. If she loved me, she'd tell her parents, she would, you know she would. She wouldn't care if they rejected her.')

'But now I've got to defrost a chicken that could easily have sunk the *Titanic* and do it in less than –' I look at my watch and panic '– *half an hour*! Oh dear God, come on, you're going to help me.'

Existential angst and pain fly out of the window when faced

with the far nastier prospect of Jay coming in to find the chicken's still not ready.

'Me?' Ross asks, horrified, and, 'Aargh!' he adds when I dump it on his lap. I dash over to the sink and wrestle with the hot tap. 'Unwrap it,' I beg him.

'OK.' Ross valiantly starts to fumble with it but gets nowhere. 'Ow! It's so fucking cold it's burning me. This thing's harder to unwrap than a born-again Christian. Ow! And it fights back.'

'Ouch! You *bloody* tap!' I howl, almost at the same time, as boiling hot water gushes out and scalds me from fingertips to wrist.

We look at each other and start to giggle.

'Does it have to be *chicken*?' he asks plaintively. 'Couldn't they make do with a nice, safe cheese salad? We could use this as a doorstop, it wouldn't be wasted.'

Everyone is taking exception to the chicken, which is going to be delicious if it kills me.

'Right,' I say and I pick it up and plunge it into a sink full of water so boiling it's probably instantly defrosted. I dust off my hands. 'That's that, then.'

We look at each other almost apprehensively.

'Don't tell me, I know,' Ross murmurs.

'... That was the easy part,' we say together.

'Wouldn't it be nice,' I mumble, reaching for the alcohol, pushing a bottle of beer towards Ross, 'if the chicken was the guest, and you ate the in-laws?'

'That, my dear,' he says, as I knew he would, 'depends entirely upon the in-laws.'

We clink bottles ironically.

I wouldn't eat mine. Too old and far too tough.

Six

It's now six pm, and they should be here any minute.

Everything is sparkling, every remotely gay decoration has been taken down, the hand towels in the bathroom are spanking clean and I'm forbidden to touch them. A magnificent chicken dinner is simmering, the smell permeating the whole flat. My stomach is doing a tarantella in anticipatory celebration.

'They should be here by now,' mutters Jay, who's even more on tenterhooks than I am.

'Relax!' I snap, and look at my watch for the third time in two minutes. 'They are precisely one minute late!'

'Then you agree that they are late?'

Oh God!

'You twerp! I love you.' And I do, when she is vulnerable and *sharing* it with me. I look at her, all tense and twanging and adorably cute, and the link between us tightens. I walk quickly towards her, breathe in her scent (laundry detergent, Natrel deodorant, Opium and her) and I hold her, breathe her in, and I want, suddenly, fiercely, to merge with her, to make her notice me, *need* me. It feels as if I'm falling into her. I look up and kiss her gently, feeling her soft lips part under mine, gently letting me in, giving and taking in a perfect dance of accord. I feel her tongue, so familiar, so wanted, explore my mouth in a sweet invasion, as I blend with her. I close my eyes, feel her breathing, smell her, and all is softness and completeness. I merge with her. I am dizzy when we pull away, yearning for more. She looks at me intensely and says, 'I love you, too.'

'Good.' And I pull her close again. The kiss grows fiercer, desire starts to whirl me away. We break apart laughing, then stop. Silence grows between us.

'You're the most important thing in my life,' Jay says suddenly, her voice urgent. 'I don't know what I'd do without you...'

The cord tightens again, pulling me in further.

'Ssshh,' I murmur, and kiss her gently again, just on the lips, feeling the softness as tenderness. I almost want to cry. I pull back and laugh – shakily – instead. I look into her eyes, try to see her soul, try to impart to her how much we two are tangled together, and how beautiful it is.

'I love you so much... so *much...*'

There is always an urgent subtext to this. Read: 'I love you so much, you *can* trust it, relax in it, let it take you over. Let me in.'

I push her hair back, frustrated because I can sense, still, how very far away from me she is, that even now, after six years, we are still having to push back the invisible enemy encroaching on us. I don't even know what that enemy is.

'Me too,' she says now and pulls me in for another kiss. I'm surrendering to the moment, when we hear a faint noise that signals 'parents'. It's the sound of a car coming too close to the front door to be that of a stranger, its door slamming, the unmistakable sound of suitcases being dragged and elderly voices coming up the path, getting closer.

Jay pulls back and pushes me away so strongly that I stagger and fall back on the couch. Off she bounds, faster than she's moved all day. The front door is flung open, letting the brisker air in. I sit up, blink a bit and try to get back into the mode that was once almost permanent, before we moved in together and I could hop in and out at will during their bloody frequent visits, the mode of greeting them as 'their daughter's best friend'.

I hear the murmur of dulcet Irish tones as I would the rumble of a distant army and there's Jay, her voice both the lit pillar of my sanctity and an unknown part of the enemy, all at once: 'Hi! Mam, Dad, come in. I'll take that, Dad, how was your journey?' And somewhere just behind consciousness, I cringe.

Parental murmurings of 'Good to see you, love' are coming towards me. I stand up, walk round in a little circle, fix the already perfect cushions. I take one panic-stricken look in the mirror, and they're upon me.

'Hi.' I smile, hopefully welcomingly.

'Hello, Miranda,' says Nora, coming forward and kissing me warmly. 'Nice to see you again.'

For the third time today, I want to cry, to lie down and yelp at the pain.

'Thanks, you too. Hello, Jim.' Kiss, kiss.

'How've you been, lass?' asks Jim paternally, after my kiss. Jim is a short man, with dark hair, dark, dancing Irish eyes and a large beer belly. He generates an immense energy and has a huge appreciation for life. One of the 'life's a party, let's enjoy it' brigade, only in a gentle, twinkly sort of way.

'Fine, thanks, yourselves?'

Jay is fussing with the suitcases like a mother hen. Any minute now she'll flap into the air with her desperate attempts to force normality on us by activity.

'Oh, we've been all right, eh?'

'Yes, indeed, Miranda, we've been fine.'

'Good!'

'I'll just put your cases in your room then –'

'Oh, thanks, Juliette,' says Nora, as wonderingly grateful as if Jay's just offered to repaint the whole room for them. What is it about parents with grown-up children? It's as though they've been doing it for so long, they've got 'parent' going all the way through them, even with each other they're primarily 'Mam' and 'Dad'. So cosy. I perch on the edge of the sofa, trying to look interested and alert.

'Don't be silly, Mam. Now, are you hungry?'

'Ah, yes, a wee bit, eh Jim?'

'Aye, I wouldn't say no to something, Jay.'

'Excellent,' Jay says, briskness concealing her fear. 'We'll eat right away then.'

'Aye, that'd be nice,' says Nora, 'if that's all right with Miranda.'

My cue has come. I jump up and head purposefully kitchenwards. 'Of course,' I call back jollily, 'I'll just go and set the table.'

'I'll give you a hand.'

'Don't be silly, Mam, you and Dad sit down, have a drink...'

I do a polite U-turn. 'What would you both like?'

Jim would like a beer, Nora a small dry sherry '... if you've got one, pet.'

Thanks to my shopping trip this morning, we do. And bloody heavy it was to carry back, too, clanking against my legs the whole way.

I assure Nora that, when it comes to sherry, we are as well stocked as Spain itself, and turn again for the kitchen. I shove the drinks on the tray, looking for perfection, then check the chicken. Beautiful. Its day-glo yellow has turned to gold, its smell delicious, its meat tender and juicy as any fowl's ever was. It's done.

I inhale with smug satisfaction, then switch the oven off. Picking up the tray, I walk carefully out, in time to hear Juliette asking if they managed to get anything to eat on the way down.

'Yes,' Nora is saying, 'we stopped off at a hotel. We had a lovely bit of chicken.'

Seven

At least she eats it. Everyone eats it, the table looks lovely, the big bowl of salad a splash of colour, the glasses sparkling, knives and forks aligned perfectly, everything shining softly in the candlelight. We've all eaten well, had some decent conversation, and, while still not completely relaxed, I am getting there. Even the sofa-bed looks gentler.

Jim pushes his chair back and sighs with satisfaction. 'Well, that was a lovely dinner, Juliette and Miranda, thank you.'

Juliette and Miranda. Tragedy and comedy. But if Jay had woken up and found her lover dead in the crypt, instead of weeping in horror, sheathing the dagger in her breast, etc, she'd have raised her eyes to heaven, given the corpse a good kick, then set off for home, muttering all the way about incompetence. Mind you, she'd never have been in that situation in the first place: Romeo could have fucked off from the start. None of that '... and all my fortunes at thy feet I'll lay...' for her. Romeo would have got: 'No, I couldn't possibly upset Mummy and Daddy.' Speaking of which...

'Yes, it was, girls. Now, we'll do the washing-up,' states Nora. Jim shoots a horrified look at his wife, but Jay is already on the case.

'You will not, Mam. Miranda and I'll do it.'

Oh yeah? After shopping for the dinner, cooking it and putting up with Jay's tantrums, all to entertain her parents, from whom I constantly have to hide one of the most fundamental parts of my nature, in case it offends them, I'll bloody wash up too?

'Of course,' I simper. 'No arguments.'

'Well, this is lovely,' sighs Nora. 'You are spoiling us.'

'Don't be silly,' coos Juliette.

'It's a lovely flat you've got here.'

'Thanks,' we say in unison and then I bite my tongue, because in their eyes it's Jay's flat and I'm just the lodger. Jay casts me a look of anguish, but they've noticed nothing. Nora is wittering happily that we can 'be totally independent here, not like when I was a girl. No, then you had to stay home with your parents until you got married. Now, it's the other way around... children only seem to stay at home until they're old enough to leave it.'

I think she may have had too much wine. Judging by the slightly embarrassed looks of her daughter and husband, they're thinking the same thing.

'Aye,' blusters Jim now, desperately trying to drag her back into the 21st century, 'but the young ones today like to be independent, Nora.'

'Oh, I know, and it's a good thing really, as long as they don't lose touch completely.'

'Mam! I come home every couple of months!' Jay protests, as well she might, considering that 'home' is in County Cork and not exactly a day trip.

'Oh, I know, I know. I wasn't talking about you, love. What about you, Miranda, do you get home often?'

Ah, here it is, the full frontal attack. Now I have to explain, and ride the politely hidden surprise of the happy family.

'About once or twice a year,' I smile warmly, trying to make that sound normal. Which it is, really. People living abroad don't see their parents in decades. The fact that mine live near Bedford is beside the point.

Yep, they're looking at me, they've sensed something out of place.

'Would your parents not like to see you more often than that?' inquires Jim.

What the hell. 'My mother probably would...'

'Miranda doesn't get on that well with her Dad,' Jay explains unnecessarily.

'No? Ach, that's a shame. Why not?'

'Dad!' Jay yelps in horror, but I find Jim's concern warming.

People don't usually care enough to ask. For the millionth time, I wonder what it would be like to have a father, a Dad, instead of the Victorian throwback I used to have, before I cut him out of my emotions forever.

'Sorry, lass,' a chastened Jim is muttering at me, 'none of my business.'

Considering I'm all but married to his daughter, it's more his business than he dreams possible.

'No, that's all right,' I pause, wondering how to continue. I gaze into my glass, swirl the remains of red wine. Fragmented scenes from the past flicker through my mind. The old buried pain stirs beneath the rubble of day-to-day consciousness.

'It's just... well, how can I put it? Oh, I know, if I were to get run over by a drunk driver, and we both ended up in hospital, Bill would visit the drunk first, to reassure him.'

I can just hear him telling the bemused man, 'No, no, it wasn't your fault... *anyone else* would have jumped out of the way.' And then he'd come and see me: 'You know, Miranda, that man's in an awful state. Couldn't you have stood a bit further back on the kerb?' tutting and shaking his head with contempt for my eternal carelessness.

'He's a decent man, and all that, and I know he'd never disown me, no matter what I did.' I glare at Jim. 'And that's the most important bit, but... we just don't get on.'

*

Indeed, we don't. The last time I was home, I thought seriously about murdering him with one of the heavy brass candlesticks my mother keeps on the sitting-room mantelpiece. I can't remember why, but he'd done or said something and there he was, sitting in his chair, snorting and sighing, and all the insults and all the tyrannies choked me. With every heavy, self-satisfied breath he took, the urge to hit him, to smash him into obliteration the way you would a cockroach, rose up in me with an intensity that was almost sexual. I actually made a move towards the candlestick and only the sudden realisation that, if I did it, it wouldn't be at all sanitary, that there'd be bits of blood and brain everywhere, stopped me. Anyway, it would have upset my mother too much: she loves those candlesticks and it would have taken her a long time to get the house back to normal after all the police and press and forensics had been over it. She doesn't even like washing up after casual visitors.

'We keep ourselves to ourselves, and they don't like it.' Bill had once patronisingly tried to explain to me why the rest of the little village hated us. Frankly, looking back, I don't blame them. I wouldn't have liked us much either. Though I wouldn't have bullied me the way the other children did, every day for seven long years.

I used to go home to *them* and that empty house where the phone never rang and no one ever popped in for a chat and it was like some simmering Tennessee Williams play that never came to the boil.

The disgusting smell of browning mince would hang heavy in the air, with Katherine crossly tending to it in the kitchen, giving it all the worry and importance other women give to cordon bleu soufflés, looking up to say only two things to me: 'Have you got homework?' and 'Have you tidied your room?'

Katherine had a great gift for making you feel she was the victim: of her husband, of her job, of the neighbourhood. She was too clever to complain. She just told you how bad so-and-so had made her feel. I grew up feeling horrendously sorry for my mother and horrendously responsible for her. Throughout those years, Bill doubtless had the same emotions. There was no warmth from either of them, no comfort and no help. When I told them about Jay, I genuinely didn't mind if they told me never to darken their door again, and I couldn't understand why other children cared so.

Only when I went to stay with Jay for the first time and saw what family could mean, did the penny drop. I was twenty-three.

Ironically enough, neither Bill nor Katherine disowned me over Jay. I've got floorboards in my parents' house, a solid foundation in a freezing cold place, with neither walls nor roof.

Jay's got solid walls, as it were, and cosy furnishings and there's a blazing fire in the hearth, but the foundations are fragile.

I suppose I'd rather have mine. Having nothing to lose does breed a certain freedom.

'And you've got no brothers or sisters?' Jim is asking, leaning towards me, his face crinkled with honest concern. I skim forward, through the pain of recollection to the nightmare present of Jay's family, with all their lies and fear and deceptions, who are waiting expectantly for me to answer the question.

'No, just me,' I beam.

'Ach, that's a shame. You must've been lonely sometimes.'

'Dad! You can't say that.'

'No, it's OK, really,' I smile, 'and anyway, Jay's almost like a sister to me now.'

'Aye, but it's not the same, is it?

'Well, no.'

He's right. Had I a sister, I very much doubt that I would be having regular sex with her. Well, I hope I wouldn't, although we might have been tempted, just for the warmth.

Anyway, what is Jim trying to do to me here? Depress me into an early grave?

'We always wanted a big family, didn't we, Nora?' he confides now, leaning back comfortably in his chair and taking out a cigar. 'Anyone mind if I –?'

'No, go ahead,' Jay and I chorus, and conversation stops while he does the whole lighting and puffing thing while we (the ladies) sit in watchful silence. What with the candlelight and the patriarchal air of the evening, the talk of families and my bowing to older authority, the impression of Victoriana is heightened surreally.

The cigar safely launched, Nora clearly thinks it's safe to relax from the edge of her chair and resume conversation.

'Aye, yes, but not everyone's the same, Jim,' she says, waving away a cloud of cigar smoke. 'Big families,' she adds, seeing our puzzled faces. 'We were talking about big families.'

I rewind the conversation. 'No, I think my parents did want more, but... it just never happened.'

'They're quite old, aren't they?'

'*Dad*!' yells Jay, putting her head in her hands, embarrassed by her parent to screaming point. She looks up again, gestures in despair at her mother, and they laugh together with all the fondness of women for the much-loved man of the house. Jim understands this, and that's why he isn't at all abashed, the way Bill would have been.

'He's seventy-six and she's sixty-six,' I snap, suddenly cross at them for daring to be happy and at ease with each other in a way that my family never were.

'Same age as you and Mam,' Jay says cheerfully. One of the many things we've got in common is elderly parents.

'Quite like indeed,' Jim agrees, peaceably, 'and you've no aunts or uncles or any close family?'

This is getting ridiculous. 'Well, a couple of aunts and cousins, but we don't really get on with them.'

All Katherine's family are dead. She probably got them to kill each other. The few that are left are Bill's sisters and their children and I've met them about ten times in my entire life. His old bitch of a mother was never interested in me and the others are only 'family' with each other, making us the outsiders. Domestic and cosy on the outside, hard inside, they're like stone covered in flour.

'So it's just me and my elderly parents, in our little village,' I squawk cheerfully.

'And do you get on with the neighbours?'

Living mewed up in that prim house with its too-neat front garden and never going out because their children would have attacked me, I don't recognise the neighbours when they stop me in the street to ask how I'm doing. I'm forever having detailed conversations with strangers and afterwards belting back and ask Katherine who they might be. Strangely, for one who claims she hates most of them and never goes out, she usually knows exactly who's who.

If this was an interview with my prospective parents-in-law so they could vet me for any possible strangeness, I don't think I'd have passed it.

Fortunately, I'm saved from having to mislead Jim yet again (by saying something like 'Oh yes, the neighbours are very friendly') by Jay, who yells '*Dad*!' again in a manner that can't be ignored.

'What?' Jim is slightly amused, slightly aggrieved. 'I'm just trying to take an interest.'

'Like a scientist takes an interest in a microbe?'

'No.' Then to me, 'But you're happy, aren't you, lass? You're not lonely?'

This is said with such genuine paternal concern that to my horror I think I'm going to cry.

'No,' I gulp, as briskly as I can, 'but that really is sweet of you to ask. Thank you.' There is a slight pause, while they all look at me, smiling, before I manage to squeak, 'Would anyone like coffee? Mrs Barrie?'

'Call me Nora, lass, and yes, I'd love a cup of coffee. Pay no mind to Nosey here.' She jerks her head at her sheepishly grinning husband. 'He means well, but doesn't know when to stop.'

'No, it's fine,' I laugh. 'Really, Jim, it was nice of you to ask.'

'Hope I didn't upset you?'

'Not at all.'

'You just don't seem to have that many people in your life...'

At the combined yells of '*Jim*!' and '*Dad*!' he jumps, and squeezes my hand. Everyone is laughing, Jay shaking her head in sweet despair.

'Wouldyoulikeacoffee?' I garble, touched and warmed, and

desperate to get away before I do or say the wrong thing and make these people, who have been so nice to me, realise, as Bill always realised, what a useless waste of space I am, and before the warmth stops, as it always does.

The thought that they might change for another reason – because they find out I am gay – doesn't cross my mind. Something like that had no effect on Bill's behaviour. If I left crumbs on the counter, though, or water on the bathroom floor, well, that was his cue to come charging at me, bellowing that I was mad and should be locked up.

'A coffee'd be great, thanks, lass,' says Jim, leaning back comfortably in his chair, with clearly no intention that things will ever change. I am comforted by this to the point of utter relaxation and the iron bar in me lifts a little, letting in the warmth.

'OK. Juliette?'

'Yes, please.'

'Four coffees coming up.' I beam inanely. At the door, I look back and see the three of them, safe in the pool of candlelight, talking and laughing in perfect accord. Nora is saying, 'Jim! That poor girl!' before slapping him, laughingly and lovingly, on the shoulder. Jay leans in towards her mother and says something that has them both in hysterics. Jim is standing his corner, saying, 'Aye, well, I'm just getting to know Jay's friends, woman, you should do the same,' in his deep, rumbling voice. Jay leans over to kiss him, then they glance up at me and I flee to the kitchen.

I kissed Bill once, in a rare moment of trying to trust, trying to love him. He was asleep at the time (which explains why I dared) and my softest of soft kisses on his lips was sufficient to wake him up with a jump.

'You know, Miranda, that was a stupid thing to do. You don't kiss someone when they're asleep. You just gave me one hell of a fright...' He raged on, while I sat, numb with fear and humiliation, at his feet.

The actual worst bit about it was Katherine, standing solemnly by, smiling her Mona Lisa smile, probably getting off on it. She never did anything to stop him: not when he came roaring out of the bathroom straight down the hall toward me, clad only in his Y-fronts (his old man's drooping bulge and sticking-out white chest hair a memory that will haunt me forever) to howl at me for leaving bathwater drips on the floor, nor when he told me I was so stupid I couldn't even answer the telephone properly, after I'd got my first-ever summer job, aged seventeen (much to Katherine's disapproval – for a time I seriously wondered if there was something wrong with me, so great was her desire to keep me indoors) and was feeling like a normal member of the human race.

I make the coffee, and manage to stop thinking about them.

And so the pleasant evening continues until, with hugs and kisses and thanks all round, we go to bed.

'Goodnight, Mir,' Jay whispers half an hour later, looking down from the sofa-bed at me on the truckle bed.

'Night, hon. Sleep well.'

'You too.'

Yeah, right.

Eight

Next day, we all go out for dinner. Very nice, very relaxed. We get back about ten-thirty.

'Right!' Jay rubs her hands purposefully. 'Everyone sit down. Mam, Dad, can I get you a drink?'

'Yes, thanks, dear; something cold, if you've got it.'

'Of course we do. Dad, what about you?'

'Oh, I'll have a Guinness, thanks, love.' No need to ask if we've got that – Jay drinks nothing else.

'Coming up, coming up,' and off she heads.

'What about me?'

'You've got legs.'

'Unlike your parents, you mean?'

'Hmmph,' and she retreats, for some mysterious reason, into her shell. We make the drinks in stony silence.

At least Jim appreciates it. 'Aaaaahhh,' he sighs, after one draught that empties half the pint, 'This is the life, eh? Now, what your mother and I thought we'd do tomorrow is a bit of sight-seeing and then go to a show.' I look studiously into my drink in case they catch me gazing at them and think I'm hinting.

'Now, we know that sight-seeing with a couple of old buffers probably isn't your ideal way of spending a Saturday –'

'Thank you dear,' interjects Nora mildly.

'One old buffer and the beautiful woman he's with.' Jim changes track as smoothly as if he's coated in Castrol GTX. 'But we'd like you both to come with us to the show. We thought maybe *Cats*... if we can get tickets? Or whatever's available.'

They never book in advance, preferring the pot-luck approach, a philosophy that landed them both boggle-eyed once at an advance showing of *Hair* in the sixties. Funnily enough, it didn't make them change their method, but they've never got that lucky again.

I'm chuffed to bits that they've included me. 'That is really kind. Thank you, I'd love to come... if you're sure I won't be in the way, you know, family...'

'Don't be silly,' snaps Jay, as well she might.

'Exactly!' booms Jim. 'So you're both coming. That's great!'

We're all sitting there beaming at each other, harmony positively sizzling between us, and I'm thinking how I've misjudged this delightful elderly couple, when there's a knock at the door. I go. It's Ross, wearing the campest outfit I've ever seen on him, which means the campest outfit I've ever seen on anyone: a pale pink flowered shirt, a fuchsia tie that exactly matches the petunias on it, beautifully ironed chinos, no socks and loafers with tassels. Pink power beads and a slim silver ring complete the picture. He's slightly drunk.

'I've got a lavender scarf that would set that off a treat,' I say.

'Fuck you!'

'Come and meet the in-laws,' I whisper. Then, 'Nora, Jim, this is Ross.'

'Hello-o,' Ross beams, shaking hands flamboyantly. Jim and Nora smile stiffly, looking like little kids whose party's just been gatecrashed by big bullies. Wariness has shuttered them off.

'So you're Juliette's dear ones. Nice to meet you at last, I've heard –' agonising pause, Jay glares at him '– the odd thing about you. Well, sorry to break up the happy little gathering. I just popped in to say, Robert and I are going away unexpectedly for the weekend – so romantic, isn't it?'

I glance at Jim in horror and see Jay doing the same. The teddy-bear look has quite disappeared. Now, he looks like a grizzly and it's a lot easier to see why Jay's so afraid of telling him that she's a lesbian.

Ross burbles on, 'So would you be a pair of poppets and keep an eye on the flat for us, you know, water the mail, stack the flowers, that sort of thing?'

He's been reading Stephen Fry again.

'Of course we will. That's no trouble. Where are you going?'

I'm being as warm as I can, but it's hard to concentrate with Jim two feet away, looking ready to explode.

'Brighton! The archetypal dirty weekend! Such fun. Well, must dash – nice to meet you –' he waves vaguely in their direction. Nora smiles faintly and nods at him, but Jim can only manage a sort of grimace, which is noted by us all. A couple of nails shoot through our bright pink balloon of friendliness and Ross's expression hardens slightly.

'Ye-es,' he drawls, 'I –'

'Well, have a lovely time, both of you,' I yell brightly, feeling like Hyacinth Bouquet, and rush over to hug him, whispering 'Sorry, Sorry!'

He shakes his head in disgust – at them, I hope. 'Thanks. You, too.'

'Thanks.' I stumble. Ross makes a move. 'I'll see you out,' I say and we reverse towards the door, smiling regally, scared to turn our backs lest we feel the *snick* of the knives going in.

'Bye, Jay,' sings Ross.

'Bye. Have a nice time,' she says tightly.

'Thanks.' Ross looks at her parents. 'It was... er...' and he stretches the pause out, making it clear that 'nice to meet you' wasn't the case. Good for him.

The second he's out the door, it starts.

'Well, he seems like a nice boy,' Nora says awkwardly.

'Oh, he is.' Jay rushes in eagerly, desperate for them to see that. 'He really is.'

Her parents look at her doubtfully. There's a rather tense silence.

I fill it with a hearty, 'Where were we? Oh yes, the theatre...'

'In a minute, Miranda,' Jim intones.

For all his faults, Bill would never make such a fucking drama over a visit from a gay neighbour. Hell, Katherine lets him invite so few people round, he'd be happy with a visit from a Jehovah's Witness.

'Jay, did I get this right... he was meaning this "Robert" was his... boyfriend?'

Jay pauses for a second before saying, 'Yes.'

There is yet another uneasy silence. Jay is squirming. She's not the only one, but I am furious. And curious, and slightly titillated: I've heard about it, I've read about it, I've watched it on TV, but this is my first-ever encounter with unabashed homophobia. I feel distanced from it, probably because it's not *my* father reviling what I am.

'Do you have much to do with them?' Jim inquires, and it's pretty clear where this is going.

'A bit.'

'Well, you know what your mother and I think of "people like that"?'

'Yes, I do.'

Jim is revving up now, 'It's not natural, it's not right. God didn't make man to go with man.'

I glance at Nora, wondering what she thinks about all this.

'Don't have too much to do with him, dear,' she simpers. 'You either, Miranda. It's not the sort of thing you girls want to have here, in your home.'

Oh my God. I look at Jay, who is looking at the floor.

'They're both very nice, Mam,' she says on a pleading note I've never heard before, 'very good people. They've helped us out a lot, haven't they, Miranda?'

'Yes,' I say strongly, 'and –'

'Well, I think you should cut the ties a bit, then,' interjects Jim, finishing off his Guinness. 'These aren't the people we brought you up to associate with, Juliette. They're unnatural and corrupt and I personally find the whole thing disgusting. Ugh!' and he actually shudders. Not one of those pissy, nancy little 'ughs' for Jim. This tremor shakes his whole manly frame and he clearly feels it's made most of his point for him. Which it has, but still he continues, 'Even thinking about it makes me feel sick... two men together...'

Why do people always say that? The thought of him and Nora 'together' doesn't please me much, but I'd never actually say so, and I certainly wouldn't let my thoughts dwell on it the way Jim's doing now, if his furrowed brow and dramatically nauseous expression are anything to go by.

Again, I think of Bill. He and Katherine also think it's unnatural and 'against God's will', but they'd never in a million years behave like this and certainly not about someone who's just paid us a friendly visit.

'It's just not the way it's meant to be,' chirps Nora.

'Thank God no child of mine turned out to be that way inclined, boys or lasses.'

I daren't look at Jay.

'No, they didn't,' smiles Nora, the perfect image of a gentle, smiling granny. 'We've got a family to be proud of.' All she needs is the knitting and it's Miss Marple to the life. Minus the keen detective skills.

I give up and look at Jay. She is grimacing awkwardly, trying to look the way a disagreeing heterosexual would. My heart, bleeding for her, turns over.

'What would you do if one of your children *had* turned out to be "that way inclined"?' I ask unctuously.

There is another slight pause, as though a breeze has gone by, ruffling their composure.

'I don't really know,' Nora says with distaste. 'I suppose we'd still love them, but it would be... difficult, wouldn't it, Jim?'

'I don't even want to think about it. I don't even know if I could talk to any of my kids again if I thought they were doing something so revolting. I'd feel... no, I don't want to talk about it, Miranda.'

I have to try. 'OK. But why be so sure it's disgusting? You really don't seem to know too much about it… how could you?' I smarm again, trying to butter over their loathing. 'But there are plenty of gay people in the city, leading perfectly decent lives.'

'No life could be decent when it's got such a central flaw. Now, can we please talk about something else? Something pleasant, like you two? And what a nice place you've got here.'

'Yes, I was meaning to say,' Nora chips in, showing more animation than she's done all night, 'it's so cosy. There's a real homey atmosphere.'

I look at her, and smile wanly. 'Thank you very much,' I say.

'Thanks, Mam, Dad.'

What would we say if they flung dog shit at us, smeared it on our walls? 'What lovely desecration? No, you feel free, go ahead, do. I insist.'

Nine

Sunday, the day of departure, eventually comes. As we gather in the sitting-room for the goodbyes, I try to look sad.

'Well, goodbye, Miranda.' Jim hugs me. 'Thank you for having us.'

'Not at all, it was a pleasure.' Now that they're going, in common with hosts the world over I find it much easier to like them.

'Yes, thank you, dear. We had a lovely stay.' Hug hug.

'Oh, thank you,' I mutter into Nora's shoulder, 'and thank you both for *Les Miserables*. I'd never have gone there otherwise...'

'It was good, wasn't it?'

'Superb!'

And then, goodbyes to me over, there is a pause while emotions move up a gear for the Major Farewell. Jim, arms held out like Topol, quavers the appropriate mantra: 'Well, goodbye then, Jay.'

'I'll just take these to the car,' I say, picking up two very heavy suitcases and making a speedy getaway as three faces quiver.

The last thing I hear is Jim saying, 'Come and see us soon, yeah? We don't see enough of you.'

Five minutes later, we wave as their car pulls out, joins the other traffic, turns the corner and is gone. Excellent! Now we can be a couple again, I exult, as we trail indoors again. Now we can do the snuggly thing of rejoining each other and talking about the relatives and the visit as a pair.

I put my arm round her. 'OK, that went well...'

Jay doesn't respond at all, and I get the feeling she'd rather my arm was nowhere near her. Coupledom is clearly out the window.

'Jay?'

She stirs. 'Yeah... yeah it did.'

'They were quite sweet really,' I concede. Nothing. I try desperate measures: 'Come here and gimme a kiss!' I want to be close to her so much, to confirm that she has given herself to me and grown away from her parents. 'Jay?'

She turns slightly and gives me a quick peck on the cheek, the sort you'd give some old guy who's been pestering you, who's maybe done something nice. I turn into it nonetheless, put my other arm round her and kiss her on the lips, trying to arouse desire, warmth... something. Again, she doesn't respond, pulls away as fast as she can. Not roughly, but it feels as though she's ripping through something as she goes, tearing the pathway of my reaching for her. I gasp.

She picks up her coat. I watch, feeling we're in parallel dimensions. I can see but not touch her and the disappointment at still being on my own is acute.

'Right. I'll see you later,' she says, as though I *am* just a flatmate. As though we don't share a soul as well as a flat.

'Where are you going?' My voice is higher than usual.

'Just out. Is that a problem?'

'Suit yourself!'

'I will!' and out she goes.

I make a desultory effort to tidy up, but the pain and panic fluttering round in me send me in ten directions at once, so that I jerk and swivel like a malfunctioning robot.

In the end I give up and go to lie on our bed, breathing in the scent of Nora and Jim (Old Spice, Sandalwood talc, *L'Air du Temps* and Pond's Cream – the scent of the contented elderly). I'm too tense to cry. Pain and panic are trying to tell me how little she loves me and it takes all my energy just to lie fallow and keep the chasm away.

But it gets better. Gradually Jay relaxes, as time smooths away the ripples of the visit and the old-fashioned ambience blends back to modern tolerance. Two days later, normality is totally resumed as we christen both the sofa and the truckle bed.

But it's not sex that makes me feel closest to her: it's the rare occasions when she opens herself up to me completely. It's now nine-thirty, Tuesday night. We're lying on top of the bed, curled into each other, my head nestled on top of her breast, our arms around each other. I move, trying to get closer still to her, to merge. Our auras, souls, join together, flatten into each other, become the sum of both our parts. I feel it joyfully expand, luminous colours burning, then stretch, replete and relaxed. *Now part of me's rejoined me...* and the colours glow joyously.

We lie like that for a while, as though taking in nourishment.

'Mmmmm,' I murmur, 'let's just stay here...'

'OK,' she says dreamily.

'No work.'

'OK.'

'No worries?'

'No worries...'

'Together whatever, whatever happens?' I say, reinforcing certainty.

Jay holds me tighter. 'Of course.'

'Good,' I say sleepily.

She kisses the top of my head. I snuggle against her, make a small noise of contentment and drift off in her arms.

How can I ever doubt it, when it's like this?

*

I sail through work the next day, buoyant and full of confidence. People get their tickets, their hotels, their dream holidays, thanks to me, and I – I am loved, I am loved and my lover is my everything, my foreign land, my homecoming.

Living only to get back to her, ridiculously sure of my welcome, I race out the door at five to five, rush to the tube, sit impatiently, willing it on through the stops – Russell Square, Holborn... half glaring, half beaming at the other passengers, until we reach – Baron's Court! I leap out, rush up the stairs and run home, feeling the magic twinkle from last night around me, and desperate to get back to her and into that other dimension again.

Panting, I insert my key in the door.

She's in the sitting-room. My heart swells, reaches. I walk in, fling my briefcase on the couch. 'Hi, gorgeous,' I say warmly.

Jay's down on her hands and knees, dusting. She doesn't say anything.

'I'll try again... hello, gorgeous!'

She doesn't look round. 'Have you seen the furniture polish anywhere?'

My heart stops for a second. It can feel the sheet of ice poised to descend on it, freezing it alive.

'No!' I snap back, angry at the pain.

'Well, would you mind looking for it? Or is that too difficult for you?'

'I will in a minute. I've just got in,' I say as lightly as I can, pretending that I've still got the right to be a human, that she's not shoved me back to donkey status.

A large, garish 'Thank You' card from her parents is on the bookcase.

'Fine. Fine,' snaps my lover of last night, still on hands and knees, with her back to me. It's like one those scenes from a nightmare, when your mother turns into Jack the Ripper. 'I should've known it was a waste of time asking you to do anything.'

'What?'

'I always have to do the clearing up around here... I have to do every bloody thing.'

'Oh shut up!' I rage, having to push through fear to do it, to claim equality, but feeling some relief from the anger when I do. 'That is just not true. You are such a drama queen. Oh!' I end, on a soft, imploding note of pain, as she throws the *Penguin Book of Lesbian Short Stories* and a sheaf of my work papers at me. I flinch as the book hurtles towards me and it hits the inside of my arm as I turn away. The papers separate and fall surprisingly violently, white feathers, white doves coming down. And I feel it is my fault, that they are accusing me as they rain down, helpless. How the fuck do women cope when it's a child?

I fall to my hands and knees to pick them up. They're horribly crumpled. Jay stands motionless, tensed for action, looking down on me. The sun's turned her silhouette black. She could be made of stone.

'Could you get these things out of here, please?' she says politely and with enormous contempt. Then she moves swiftly to the couch and flings my briefcase onto the floor in one sweeping movement that speaks of enormous, bottomless rage held in check. 'And *this*.'

The depth of the difference between this and what I was expecting is the depth of the pain I feel now.

It's as if I'm trying to sunbathe in the Arctic, only the Arctic's too nice and friendly for this. Siberia, where the salt mines are, where they take the prisoners. That's it, and anyone dumb enough to try sunbathing in Siberia deserves all the pain they get.

But we were so *together* last night.

'Why are you being like this?' I whisper.

'Like what?' she sneers, *condescendingly*, putting herself far above the bond between us that would make such behaviour unthinkable. 'Just because I don't want to live in a *pigsty*...' and then rage sweeps through her. 'And what's *this* doing here?' she screams, as she hurls a mug that's dared to be there since last night at me. I am terrified of her when she's like this, terrified and enraged at the betrayal.

'It's a *mug*,' I yell at her (and in my mind I'm saying 'It's a *chicken*...' over and over again). 'It's my mug, I live here t–' The words die in my throat as I see what she is doing. Blind with fury, in a hideously methodical way, she is throwing all the little trinkets that are mine onto the floor. Down goes a fat black pottery pig I'm very fond of, smashed to smithereens with a hideous crunch and, ridiculously, I ask, 'Could you please be *careful,*' as though I'm the lady of the manor talking to a removal man. Then reality kicks back in and, yelling, *'How dare you, you arrogant bitch!'*, I march up to her, shaking, and grab her arm. It's like grabbing the branch of a huge tree flinging about in a gale. She simply shrugs me off, goes back to her manic 'tidying up'.

'I don't know why I bother with you,' she hisses, her lips stretched into a thin line with the effort of keeping the rage under control.

I know she's not going to be able to contain it for much longer and am flattened to white stillness.

'You're nothing but a lazy, spoiled little girl who can't be bothered to keep things neat and tidy,' she screams, frenziedly throwing the little figures onto the floor. The crashing reverberates around me.

Then she flings down the photo of Katherine, Bill and me and, without thinking, I yell, 'Be *careful!*'

'Of *what*? Of all the things you leave for me to keep clean and tidy? You don't even *care* about them, or you would make more of an effort.'

I have no idea whether she means my possessions or my

parents. I whisper, through the bar in my throat, 'That is just not *true*.'

Then she turns to the little music box my parents gave me on my thirteenth birthday, which is now a bit chipped and worn and which she's always felt didn't belong in the sitting-room.

'And why do you keep this, anyway? Stupid-looking thing... we should throw it out. Yes, let's throw it out *right now*.' And she rushes to the kitchen with it.

I will myself to be calm, knowing that I can't stop her, but all the same feel that I'm making a sacrifice to propitiate a Fury.

I'm just glad she's out the room.

I know it's sick but at least when she's furious with me, I know I have her full attention. There is more dignity in being yelled at and (occasionally) hit, than there is in being shut out. This way, she's in it as much as I am.

Lethally quiet, she comes back. Adrenalin surges again. I'm being flooded with the damn stuff. It can't be good for me. Like dirty water, when it goes down, it'll leave a ghastly residue.

Desperately hoping she hasn't thrown my box away, I ask, 'What did you do with it?'

'What do you think?' she snaps.

Denying to myself that she could hurt me so, my voice cracking with misery and tension, I ask, 'Did you throw it away?'

She ignores me and goes back to the dusting.

'*Did you throw it away*?' I scream suddenly, and she jumps.

Tension trembles in the air, as we both wonder if this has pushed the rage loose.

Still she says nothing, and suddenly her answering has become a test of my worth. I look bleakly at her turned head, and wonder how she can do this to me.

Much, much later, I would realise that she had been trying to break me down, blend me into the ground so that I wouldn't forever be popping up as a threat.

Never give yourself completely to anyone whose parents don't dance to the Ballad of Unconditional Love. Their anger at such parents is too painful for them to acknowledge and it wends its way beneath their anger at themselves. Tread carefully around such people, for they will destroy you unthinkingly to preserve the emotional status quo, in which their parents' measure of them is the correct one.

But I didn't realise this until it was all over.

'It's in the bin, yes!' she states, her voice a mixture of defiance and joy that she's done it. Also a smidgin of guilt, which I know will grow and take her over until she loathes herself for this monstrous behaviour, but I'm too stung by her to wait.

'You stupid, ignorant *bitch*!' I turn to go into the kitchen to rescue my box.

Jay, quick as a flash, is in front of me. She is dangerous.

'You. Are. Not. Taking. It. *Out*!'

'I bloody well am,' I whisper, my throat constricted.

'You are not going into that kitchen.'

'Stop being such a *bully*!' I know that Jay is not really a bully, that this is the monster. I am trying to reach her, to sting her back to sanity.

I push past and she grabs me and throws me down on the couch. I bounce, winded with shock as much as pain. The indignity of it hurts more than anything.

'Now *stay* there until I'm finished,' she yells, desperate for me not to count, not to matter.

I struggle up and head kitchenwards. 'Get stuffed!' I fling at her in passing, my heart beating so fast and so intensely, I think I'm going to choke.

She grabs me again, more violently than before. Her hatred and impatience soak through me as she grips my arms as though she'd like to push through them, to grind muscle and bone together, as she drives me back to the couch. I don't struggle. It's like being borne along by a tidal wave, and some instinct for survival makes me go limp. Give over independence.

Still holding my arms, she thrusts me, face down, onto the couch so violently that the shock of impact dazes me a little and gives a couple of seconds of black and starry peace, blessedly suspending the struggle to be me.

It can't last. Reluctantly I take a couple of gasping breaths, dizzily lift my head. She's looking down on me the way you'd look at a disgusting child, she the adult struggling for control over overwhelming odds.

'Now stay there, I'm *warning* you,' she growls, and I know that she is indeed warning me. If I get up again she will have no control over the monster.

It's strange to hear this hybrid of sanity and swirling rage-induced madness. And the fact that I have done nothing wrong, the fact that she can seem so superior and be so wrong, lights up in me and I get up off the couch and scream at her, 'Who the bloody hell do you think you are? You're pathetic, you stupid creep, carrying on like bloody Hitler. *Who the hell do you think you are*? You can't even get the courage to tell your parents you're gay – and the rest of your stupid family.'

I get no further because she's on me. Like an enraged tiger, bearing me to the floor, and ohhh, I had forgotten, forgotten what this was like, how horrible, how terrifying, her rage unleashed on me.

All I can do is hold my breath and try to survive it. I cover my head as best I can while she hits it, panting, 'Why do I *bother* with you? You're not worth it. This is *the end*, all right, the end, you're not *worth* it.'

It is a cry of desperation that has the ring of truth about it. I am not worth the risk of losing her family. I am not worth the effort of trying to bend her nature to share partnership with me.

I am not worth the constant struggle of trying to be something she's not.

'You're not *worth* it,' she cries again, almost in desperation, as though she had expected some rare treasure that had simply never appeared.

I cower, covering my head, feel the shame for both of us.

She continues to pound me, trying to find the places that hurt.

I hear myself screaming, 'Stop it. *Stop it...*' and then it does stop. She draws back, gasping. There is one last contemptuous swipe, then the cold draught of her getting off me.

I lie there, not daring to move or have any part of me exposed. She's won. She's made the point, can say 'Shut up' or 'Don't move' or throw my belongings away. She can do it and anything like it, because I was completely helpless to her there and I can't stand the 'punishment' that comes if I fight back. I am humiliated into the dust. Swollen patches start to throb all over my body. Back to this. Last time, about six months ago, she used a tin I collected change in to beat me with and then had to bath me for a couple of days because I couldn't lift my arms.

Waiting for the bruising, the swelling and the pain to go is disgusting. Because it's *there*, a reminder of how abnormal your relationship is. How do you forget how little your partner loves or respects you, when every bruise, every wince, is a marker of it? Then again, every bruise says, 'At least she cared enough to get angry.' A woman wrote, 'bruises like kisses'. Somewhere, in the cold clarity of sanity, I know it's disgusting, but in desperation we take whatever we can get.

I lie there, cold and empty, hollowed out, feeling to the marrow of my bones that Bill was right: there is something about me that is not worthy of being treated with love.

Jay is saying shakily, 'I told you to stay on the couch.'

This is too much. 'I'm not a bloody dog,' I snap, wearily levering myself up. She makes a sudden move toward me and, horrified, I flinch back down, quick as light, thinking frantically, 'Oh no, not again! Pleeeaasse...'

'I'm not going to touch you.'

I can feel the waves of rage, now much further out in her, flattening until they've gone. She waits, in the silent emptiness of their passing, then turns abruptly and leaves the room. It's like that peace that came when the Incredible Hulk turned back into... whoever it was. The extra presence has left us.

I wait, gathering strength, stand up shakily and take a few deep breaths. I gather more of my old self around me, pushing back shock and fear, and then, with some trepidation, finally go into the kitchen to see what's happened to my poor box. I feel like a maiden entering the dragon's lair.

In the end, it's nothing. The kitchen is mundane as ever, tainted like the whole flat by the creature's visit, but still just our kitchen. I gingerly lift up the lid and peer into the bin.

'Oh no!' I am surprised that the hurt can still be so bad, that there are still outrages. I'd expected to see it in the bin, maybe chipped a little bit more, but my lovely, loved, familiar box is destroyed. I stare at what's left, reluctant to touch it, taking in its loss. Then I lift it out gently and wander back into the sitting-room and collapse onto that bloody couch again.

Part of me is thinking, 'How ridiculous, it's only a box, you're sitting here like Lear with Cordelia,' but another part is keening softly, not just for the loss of the box, but for the way the relationship has been rent in two, revealing an underside of red anger and hatred instead of love. Part of me is just grieving for the loss of gentleness.

I lie wearily down on the couch, just as she comes back. I panic, picturing more violence, and start to struggle up, but the bruises have begun to ache and I don't get very far. She comes over and it's all right. The beast's gone and peace is back in her, along with a deep sense of shame. She pushes me gently back down, gently takes the box from me and looks at it.

'I'm sorry. I'll get you another one.'

Some of the warmth from her concern permeates and comforts me and, although I am panicking at her nearness, I feel taken care of, like a small child who's had a fright. In my quest for love, I am way beyond seeing how unfair this is.

'I don't think they're making them any more,' I say painfully.

'Oh. Well, maybe I could mend this one, then.'

I look at it. To mend it properly is going to take real skill and craftsmanship. I look at Jay.

'I don't think so.'

Suddenly, the real loss hits me, as I remember Bill and Katherine giving it to me, see their pleasure in my happiness, the care they'd obviously taken to pick it out. Jay has smashed into a piece of my history she had no right to destroy. I try to get up again but again she won't let me.

'Don't go.'

'You think I want to stay here with *you*?' I shrug off her hand, stand up and glare down at her.

She looks at me, then looks away.

'No.' She is crying tears of self-hatred. I watch her bent, vulnerable, hurt head for a full minute, feeling love push its way back in, painfully banishing righteous disgust.

'*Why* did you do it?' I finally yelp, dredging the most important question up from the morass of pain. 'Why, when everything is going fine, do you always have to ruin it?'

Juliette drops her head and starts to weep. I hardly ever see her like this – the rather butch surface cracked, pulled aside to let the other emotions out. 'I don't know,' she sobs, 'I *don't know*. Don't you think I wish I did... do you think I like being like *this*?' Words fail as pain takes her over, and she buries her wet, swollen face in her hands. She is literally heaving with grief and it's genuine, so genuine I can almost see it surround me, taste it.

And, as she's so clearly feeling the pain, I feel it lift from me, feel blessedly lighter and airier.

I smile lopsidedly at her. 'You are *sad*, do you know that?' She nods pathetically into her hands. I look at her for a second or two longer and then give in to the longing. 'Oh, come here...' and I pull her into a cuddle.

In truth, I'm not sure if the longing was to comfort her, or to crawl into her carapace, push up into it, push myself in. I am so scared of losing her and she is so easily gone, lost inside herself, shutting the world out. I always have to keep shoving myself in. One thing is sure: she will not come to me.

She is sobbing hard now, every breath a gasping effort, before she pulls away, snuffling, and tries to wipe her nose on the back of her hand. No good. I can tell she's longing to blow her nose but is too demoralised to move.

'Would you like a tissue?' I ask, painful amusement bubbling up through the raw patches in my throat. She nods pathetically. I go to the bathroom.

Subconsciously, I am resentful of all the energy being churned into the maw of this, but, right at that moment, all I am conscious of is the need to get back to her while she is still open.

'Here you are.'

She snuffles her thanks, can't stop crying. 'Oh...' I hug her, take control, borrow strength from the maternal.

'What was all that *about*?' I ask, as a mother whose child has just had a bad tantrum. Parent/child roles are being crazily swapped between us.

She shrugs that she doesn't know, a convulsive movement grabbed before weeping claims her again.

'But you *must* know,' I say, gentle as cotton wool.

'But I don't,' she jerks out. 'It's all about control, being in control, but I don't know why I'm like this...' She puts her head down. Her voice is muffled. 'I wouldn't blame you if you left me.'

I sigh. 'I'm not going to leave you.'

'You could... After this, who'd blame you?'

'Don't be silly,' I croon, 'I love you.'

'Do you?'

Love comes back softly, filling the room.

'Of course I do... more than anything...'

There is a pause.

'I love you too,' Jay cries desperately and I hold her as the tears are wrenched out of her. 'I'm sorry... I'm really sorry... I promise it will never happen again. Make as much mess as you like.'

We both laugh shakily.

'You know you couldn't cope with that.'

'No, you're right.'

The gleam of our sense of humour is back, enfolding the circle of 'us' again.

'I know,' I say, and hug her again, feeling her arms go round my waist, her wet cheek rest against my shoulder; feeling her relax into me again. Not quite as we were, not quite there yet – there is still an edge keeping her out – but nearly. I smell her damp hair, put my cheek against her hot, cracked one, hold her close, feel her re-enter me. We stay there.

'I do love you,' Jay says, her voice deep with the miracle of it all, 'I couldn't bear to lose you.'

I hold her tighter. 'You're not *going* to lose me.'

She starts to cry again.

'Ssshhhhhhhh,' I hush her. 'Sssshhhhh. It's OK. Sshhh. I know, I know…'

Ten

Jay, her concrete surface having been blasted apart by the explosion, felt free over the next few days to be softer. Without the covering, all sorts of sentimental gentlenesses came out of her and I felt that I'd found my way onto a patch of sun-warmed grass.

It couldn't last, but you never think that at the time. You think, yes, this is it, I'm here now, climbed the stile, followed all the signs and am in the meadow I always knew existed. I just had to keep trying. You think that now your partner's seen what it can be like, it'll all be easy.

And it was, for a week, until Ross and Robert's engagement party...

We take a bottle of champagne and follow the trail of music and laughter to their part of the house. It's recently been redecorated with black Habitat stuff – very dramatic. I think that's Robert. There's a trace or two of Ross to be found in the bowls of pot pourri in the hall and their guest bedroom is a dream of pink and blue, with Monet prints on the walls, but the rest of the flat's a fantasy in ebony and chrome. The huge scarlet duvet on their huge double bed is about the only splash of colour in it and certainly makes a statement.

Right now, there are about fifteen people milling around, including my good friend Arabella (early thirties, terribly posh, rather shy, very much the black sheep of her frighteningly aristocratic family after coming out about her relationship with Pamela) and Martin and his partner Will. Will is twenty-eight, very slender, rather fey, hard to get to know, definitely mischievous. Like a woodland fawn. Martin's thirty-three, very earnest, very into gay rights, thinks Peter Tatchell's on the right lines. (Actually, so do I.)

Unusually for a gay man, Martin's not terribly fashion-conscious. Bless him, he's a type – chunky shoes and serious sweaters and causes. If he were straight, he'd be a sort of 'Gavin', family man, one pint down the local twice a week, wash the Ford Escort on Sundays, talk seriously about the perils of higher taxation, the trouble their youngest is causing ('though that's more the wife's department, ha-ha') and the trouble he's having with his begonias.

As it is, he goes clubbing with Will more than he'd like to, is a regular at the gym and drives a Porsche convertible. He does grow begonias, much to Will's despair, but in a window-box. You can spot their floor a mile off.

Ross taps his glass for hush. We all gather round and gradually the babble dies to a murmur and then to that shifting silence that precedes a speech. Ross is looking as embarrassed as people who are about to address a crowd of their friends when sober usually do.

'Ahem… right then…' he starts, then takes a deep breath and goes for it. Yeah Ross!

'Well, it's true. He's finally going to make an honest man of me.' There is some drunken cheering at this point. 'Yes, I know,' he concedes, beaming, 'I feel rather like that myself.'

He reaches out and takes an embarrassed Robert's hand. 'Oh, how sweet, look, he's gone all shy. Now, my dear ones, we haven't set a date yet, but when we do, you know you're all invited… to the reception.' We boo dutifully. 'No, seriously, I just want to say how thrilled I am and how happy I am, that this man and I –' gently he strokes Robert's cheek '– this man and I are going to be together for the rest of our lives.' And they look at each other, total commitment.

I gulp, try to picture myself and Jay in that position. Why not? I know, it's the way that Robbie is looking back at Ross, total solemnity, total abandonment. With a gun at her back, I could get Jay onto the platform but, at this point in the proceedings, she wouldn't be looking into my eyes, she'd be looking off to one side, excruciatingly embarrassed.

'And that you're all going to be there to share it with us,' Ross is stuttering. 'Anyway, I just wanted to say how lucky I consider myself to be – and now I've said it. This is a terrible speech, let's get on with the party!'

We all cheer. Martin raises his glass in a toast: 'Ross and Robert!'

'Ross and Robert!' we chorus, and we have a moment of pure fellow-feeling, with everyone giving out warmth, not one single dissenting vibe in the place. We feel bathed in it and we are all grinning stupidly, when a brick shatters through the window with a crash that seems to reverberate forever. Glass flies towards us in slow motion. Faces stretch in shock.

Into the stillness a male voice, coarse with loathing, yells, 'Fucking faggots!' and the spell is broken. Martin, with an inarticulate cry, hares out the door after whoever did it and Ross, immediately wiser than the rest of us, shouts, 'Martin, *no*!' Then, 'Is everyone all right?' he yells, looking round at us, and, on seeing that we are, 'Come on, we can't let him go out there on his own.'

A vision of Martin being beaten up by a gang of homophobes swims into our minds and we move as one towards the door. It's just as well that Martin re-enters right then, or we'd probably all still be stuck in the door-frame, such was our kindled determination to rescue one of our own.

Martin is panting, and cheated of his prey. 'Whoever it was has scarpered,' he says furiously, and then he makes a bee-line towards Will.

'My hero,' murmurs the little fawn, sweeping him into an embrace.

'Little *bastards*,' spits Martin, still quivering with righteous indignation, 'little cowardly *pricks.*' There is a murmur of agreement, but most of us are too subdued to raise much wrath. We're thinking of what they *could* have done.

Ross looks round at us and tries desperately to raise the atmosphere. 'We-ell,' he drawls, camping it up, 'they *did* wait until after the speech,' and for some reason we all find this hilarious and laughter replaces horror.

'There's probably a manual out there somewhere – The Brick-thrower's Guide to Etiquette,' someone shouts.

'How to Bluff Your Way in Brick-Throwing,' screeches somebody else.

Robert picks up the brick and examines it critically. 'Hhmmm, yes, clearly you should always make sure that your brick is clean and neat at the edges – a brick, in short, to make Mother proud. Ideally, it should –'

'How can you all laugh at this?' Martin interjects furiously. 'Someone could have been seriously hurt by that piece of crap. It's not funny.'

The laughter that had been engendered by the clowning dies away. Ross goes swiftly over to him.

'Martin, dear boy –'

'Now he sounds like Noel Coward,' whispers one of the bitchier gay boys from Will's contingent.

'Shut your face,' Will mutters back.

'We know it's not funny,' continues Ross, gesturing to Robbie to turn the music up and to the rest of us to get the party going again, 'but to take it seriously is to give them what they want, to give them a significance that I *will not give them* in my life. Now, have a drink and let's help that divine little lover of yours to clean up.'

Martin calms down a little, slaps him on the back, then glances round and sees Will with Ross's dustpan in one hand and a lethally sharp piece of glass in the other and lets out a bellow like a cow who's just seen her calf wandering towards a water-filled ditch.

'Will, no! Let me!'

This causes Will, who has, unsurprisingly, leaped three feet with shock, to nearly stab himself in the heart. Martin rushes towards him, cooing.

I see Ross chuckle wryly and catch his lover's eye. They exchange glances, each checking that the other is all right. Both nod imperceptibly. I look at Jay. She is gazing at the broken window. Knowing Jay, she's probably got a sneaking sympathy with the throwers – after all, they share the same attitude as her family, only they're more pro-active.

The party's getting going again. Martin, having taken over the dustpan, has nearly succeeded in collecting all the glass. Cher is booming out of the stereo, conversation is getting going and people are starting to relax again.

Martin finishes sweeping and starts to tape up the window, fussily giving Will the tape to hold.

Ross wanders into my orbit. 'You OK?' I ask quietly.

'Yes. Shall we dance?' He holds out his arm gallantly, as though we were a lady and gentleman of the eighteenth century about to do the cotillion. I nod as graciously as I can, take his arm, and we sweep regally onto the floor and dance to Cher until our partners come up and cut in.

Jay and I, not being much good, have to sit down two minutes later. Ross and Robbie keep going effortlessly. Arabella joins us and then Martin, who now has a blood-stained hanky wrapped round his hand.

'Do any of you know where Ross keeps the first-aid kit?' he demands crossly.

Jay nods and they wander off together. Arabella turns to me.

'Wasn't that a sweet speech Ross made? And isn't it lovely, that they're making such a commitment, getting married? It really shows the strength of their feelings for each other. How long have they been together now?' Arabella's very sweet, but sometimes she's just a bit too shiny to be true. It's as though she's been kept in clingfilm all her life.

'Two years.'

'Right, an amazing show of commitment... they must love each other very much.' Slight pause. 'How are you and Jay getting on?'

'Oh, fine, thanks, fine,' I beam, on the strength of the past week.

'Any wedding bells on the horizon for you two, then?'

What the fuck is this? I feel like Bridget Jones being asked why she doesn't have a husband. All the pressure of being gay *and* all the pressure of being straight? I don't think so. I glance round the room pointedly. 'This is a *gay* party, isn't it? Only I could swear I'm at some awful cousin's straight wedding, or something.' And then some of my frustration at forever being part of a sub-group of society comes out. Poor Arabella.

'Ross and Robert won't be having "bells", Arabella, because they aren't getting "married". They're having a blessing. It means the same thing in every sense except of course the legal one, and the fact that the dear darling Church won't ring the bells after it... not unless, with perfect timing, a royal dies, or the whole town burns down, or something, the second they've taken their vows. Maybe Ross and Robert's blessing will in fact herald in something like the last days of Sodom for West Kensington... you never know... I'm sure the Church'd ring its bloody bells then.'

Silence. I'm still heaving with indignation, about more than society's recent distaste for us, so when Arabella mutters, 'Sorry I spoke,' it gives me the boost to spit out, 'And the answer to your question, Arabella, is no, there are no "wedding bells" on the horizon for Jay and me.'

More's the pity. I can just see it – Jim in a morning suit, Nora in something tasteful by Marks and Spencer, sitting in the pews while their Jay and I pledge eternal love to each other.

Arabella looks as though she's wandered into a minefield.

One false step, and she's caught in an explosion.

'Yes. Right. Fine. Sorry I brought it up,' she articulates, nerves making her sound posher and more stilted than Prince Charles among a crowd of the working classes. I come back to earth feeling guilty and grope for something positive to say.

'No, I'm sorry. Actually, Jay and I are going to go abroad together soon. It'll be our first time abroad together. Actually, it'll be our first real holiday together.'

Without thinking, Arabella blurts, 'But you've been together six years – sorry, *sorry*!'

'Yes, but Jay always has to go home for the holidays... "family".'

I'd never really brought this up before. Having adapted to it myself, I'd buried it deep. I'd turned the odd weekend away together into an epic and covered up the problem with excuses so jagged they'd have cut me if I fell on them.

'Yes, right, I see... excellent,' she stumbles, desperate to get the words out before I kill her.

'Oh God,' I say, 'I'm sorry. I've scared you, haven't I?'

'Only *completely* rigid,' she concurs, and we laugh. I squeeze her shoulder in apology and she grins at me. Arabella's lovely. And rich. Why can't I fancy *her*?

As I let go her shoulder, I see the creature I do fancy returning with a sheepish Martin, who is now sporting a large blue Band-aid on the injured hand.

'Wow!' gasps Arabella in mock amazement. 'That was some ferocious piece of glass.'

Martin looks huffy. 'This was the smallest Band-aid Juliette could find.' He spots Will. 'Excuse me...'

'Yeah, and I'd better go and find Pamela.' Arabella disappears too. Jay and I look at each other. Alone at last.

'Arabella wanted to know if there were any wedding bells on our horizon,' I say and she laughs dismissively. I glare at her. 'I should have told her, the only bell on our horizon is a handbell – the one your parents'd give us if you ever told them about us.' I mime ringing one. 'Unclean, unclean.'

'That's not funny.'

'I *know*.'

We each wait for the other to say something conciliatory. There is a considerable pause before Jay sighs sharply, 'Right. Well, if you can't say anything sensible, I'll go and talk to someone else.' And off she goes too.

'You do that,' I say defiantly, to nobody. 'Ohhhhh,' I yelp at the empty air, then look up to see Ross watching me gravely. I shrug at him and attempt a grin.

I slip away and the party continues without me. Jay, on the other hand, stays until they throw her out. She staggers into bed at three o'clock, reeking of booze – and she has the hang-over from hell in the morning.

Eleven

Relationships are full of milestones, aren't they? You remember the day you first met, the first kiss, the first time you had sex. Anniversaries, funny stories, building layers of trust on a mutual past. And always you trust that the foundations are there for you to lean on.

I remember the day our foundations gave way. It was later that year and we were planning to spend Christmas together in Tenerife. I'd been so pleased about the holiday, about spending an actual week off with her. I mean, I work in a bloody travel agent's – I have so many possibilities. I see everybody else who works there going for mini-breaks left, right and centre, even going to Florida for the weekend.

I passed up so many good deals because Jay wouldn't use her annual leave, saying that They 'wouldn't understand if I didn't go home to Ireland to catch up'. I, on the other hand, understood perfectly. So, for my own holidays, I always either went to my parents' (until I came too close to murder there) or stayed in the flat alone. I didn't want to go on holiday by myself and all my friends were in couples. But this year something changed in Jay and she wanted to spend a holiday with me, abroad. Admittedly her parents were going to Canada for Christmas to see her brother, but I still thought it was a sign that we'd turned a corner and she was leaning toward me more, them less. I felt possessive. I felt couply.

On the morning in question, I kiss her goodbye, saying I'll bring some brochures back with me. 'Ooooh, Tenerife here we come... sun, sea and sand!' I sing, dancing towards the door. Jay smiles complicitly, waving me off. As I skip down the garden path, I hear the telephone start to ring, but think nothing of it.

That night, I'm back before her, brochures spread all over the coffee table. I wave a couple of them at her when she comes in.

'Look... Tenerife: a warm volcanic island, in the blue waters of the Atlantic... drive into the hills... sample the local cuisine...' I've gone to a lot of trouble to find the perfect spot for us, far enough away from the usual tourist trails to be genuinely unspoilt; near enough to civilisation to be comfortable. 'The local wildlife is –'

'I'm not going,' Jay interrupts flatly. She meets a wall of incomprehension.

'Wh – what? Don't be silly.'

She takes off her coat slowly, drops it on a chair. 'I'm not being silly.' Her voice has no expression.

Silence.

'What do you mean, you're not going? This is a wind-up, isn't it? It is...'

'It's not a wind-up. I'm not going because my mother phoned this morning. The whole family is going to their house for Christmas because Sinead and Owen are getting engaged.' She sounds like a robot.

'What? Why didn't you say you couldn't go?'

'She is my sister.'

'Right,' I say, grappling with this changing landscape, 'so what does that make me then?'

'That makes you the woman I love.'

'Oh please.'

'*Please* try to *understand*.'

'Am I invited to this gathering?' There is a sinking silence. 'Am I?'

Finally, defeatedly, she says, 'No.'

'No.' I pace around a bit. 'I can't believe you're doing this... after all the plans we made for this stupid –' and I sweep all the brochures off the table '– holiday.'

They lie there, under the coffee table, a little pool of blue that's as deep as the ocean.

'Don't...' says Jay, from deep in her throat, as she bends down to pick them up.

'Why not? It's perfectly bloody obvious that we're never

going to do anything together as a couple. There's always going to be something. I'd understand if we'd only been together a little while, but we've been together five bloody years now. I'm never going to come first with you, am I?' I sound as bleak as I feel.

'Of course you are – you do, but come on. What else could I have done?'

'Sinead knew you were going on holiday with me that week.'

'Yes.'

'So surely she'll understand when you tell her that of course you'll be going to the wedding, but you can't just cancel a holiday and let your "friend" down, just because she suddenly decides to get engaged.'

'It wasn't like that.'

'What's she trying to do anyway – grab Owen before he has a chance to change his mind?' I loathe Sinead and the feeling's returned with interest.

'No, don't be stupid... and you know I can't do that.'

'Why not?' I demand, and here it comes, the fucking appalling joke of the whole situation, the reason I can get shoved aside on occasion after occasion, the reason couply things are forever beyond us.

'Because they think that's all you are – my friend. They wouldn't understand.'

'But I'm supposed to? I'm supposed to be all right with being totally let down – again – for them. What the hell do you think I am? Some sort of bloody non-person, whose feelings don't matter in the slightest?'

'No, of course not... it's not *like* that,' Jay cries desperately, and tries to hold me. 'We will go to Tenerife, just not this holiday.'

'Don't!' I shove her off and step back hurriedly. 'I can't believe you're doing this to me. What am I supposed to do while you're congratulating your bloody sister?'

'You can still go –'

'On my own? I can't believe you said that.'

A barren silence falls for a moment or so.

'I'm sorry. I really am. I'll make it up to you, I promise,' Jay stutters. Again, she tries to hold me, again I shove her away. The evening sky is rich and deep, perfect for lovers to be wrapped in.

'When?' I scream, 'New Year? Which happens to be my birthday.'

She just looks at me and I know what's going on.

'Ah, silly me, you'll be staying in Ireland to spend that with your *family*. If you're going to be gay, children, don't have a birthday that falls on a national holiday. Have one stuffed somewhere in the middle of the year – Tuesday to Thursday for absolute security. Let's see, February somewhere might be a good time... oh, but not Valentine's Day, or the family might wonder, and not a leap year either, because they're so *special*, *family*'s the place to spend them. February the eighth might be OK, unless it's also the birthday of a member of the family, in which case you're fucked all over again.' I grind, panting, to a halt.

'Look, I've said I'm sorry,' Jay is going from apologetic to irritated, 'and I am, and I will make it up to you.'

'You can't make this up to me,' I say, and every word is speared with pain. 'You didn't even *discuss* it with me first. You couldn't have made it clearer what you really think of "us".' To my horror I start to weep.

'That's not true,' Jay says desperately, 'You've got it *wrong*...'

Another pause, gentler than the last, ensues, caused by exhaustion and stalemate.

'All right,' I try at last, knowing what the answer will be. 'It's your only sister's engagement, very special, etc etc.'

Jay nods, 'Yes, it is.'

'Right, then let me come too.'

Another pause. I know she isn't really considering it. The decision's already been made, she's wondering how to say no.

The moon shines bright outside. Children laugh in the street.

'You know that's not really possible,' she says at last.

'No...?'

'It might be different if you'd ever got on with Sinead... or even Owen.'

Owen – fat, pastry-faced, bland, pouty and sulky, with a nasty streak. Owen laughs at other people's humiliations: an old lady slipping on a banana skin, a woman being yelled at by her husband, a child dropping its ice-cream are meat and drink to him. Would having a daughter who's gay really be worse than having one who's marrying *him*, giving you grandchildren carrying half his DNA? Silly me – of course it would. There's no logic to bigotry.

Anyway, she's lying and she knows it. 'No, it wouldn't be different,' I say, 'you still wouldn't have the guts to take me.' She says nothing. '*Would* you?' Hope flares for a minute.

'No.'

'No... You're pathetic, d'you know that? Thirty years old and you're still scared of your family.'

'I'm scared of them rejecting me, yes,' she almost yells.

'More scared of losing them than losing me?'

'I couldn't cope if they never wanted to see me again... you know that.' Yes, in other words.

'What're you going to do when your parents die? And when your brothers and Sinead are all married and concentrating on their families? What're you going to be? The family freak? Funny old Aunty Jay, nice enough to spend a day or a night with, but that's it? The relative that everyone knows there's "something funny" about, but nobody brings it up. Christ, it's like something out of the 1950s. *It's not illegal any more, you know.*'

Ornaments tinkle, the leaves of our books shiver, as my roar passes over. We let the vibrations die away.

'I know, I know,' Jay says, as tired of being trapped as I am of her being trapped. 'Everything you've said is true. When my parents are dead, I won't care about the others...'

'Your parents could live until they're a hundred and I could get run over by a bus tomorrow.'

'Yes, but that's not likely to happen, is it?'

'Which? Oh, forget it...' I take a deep breath. 'So, you're going to be at this family gathering and I'm going to be stuck here on my own.'

'Go away somewhere.'

'On my own!'

'Ask Ross, or Arabella or –'

'Right. Instead of you... oh, this is going nowhere, like "us". I'm going out.'

'Where?' she asks, slightly panicked, not wanting me to go when things are like this.

'Oh, fuck off, will you, just *fuck off*. Back to your precious fucking family, and leave me alone.' I grab my coat and slam the door behind me, taking a bitter satisfaction from denying her something she wanted.

And so, a fortnight later, we're saying goodbye in the sitting-room. Sinead's engagement party is looming. If I let myself think that we should be packing excitedly together for Tenerife, I'm done for, so I don't. Well, not much. Not more than once a minute.

'Well, have a nice time,' I utter, as graciously as I can.

'I will... you too. Have a good Christmas.'

'Oh yeah,' I utter bitterly, hating myself even as the words come out.

'I'm sorry. I can't keep on saying it.'

'I know...'

'It won't always be like this.'

'No?'

'No.'

And because I love her, because I need her, because I'm hanging in for the long haul together, I believe her.

'Oh, come here... give me a cuddle,' and I step towards her, melt into her. Bliss. 'It feels like you're falling into me. Do you feel it too?'

'Yes,' she chokes.

'What a life...'

'Yes.'

We pull apart slowly, agonisingly slowly. It feels like my first day at school, swapping warmth and safety for the chill winds of the outside world. It's hard for me to remember that Jay is actually looking forward to going home.

'You'd better go,' I say, defeated by fate, but determined to ride it nonetheless. But as she picks up her suitcase and heads toward the door, apparently unconcerned by the parting, I feel a pang deep in my heart and it's all I can do not to double over.

'I'll phone you when I get there.' The usual dreary routine.

'Yeah.' It'll be the phone call of a flatmate to her flatmate, no affection in it, no truth. When we part because she goes home, we really part. And it's agony to me.

She gives me another hug. 'I love you.'

'Yeah.'

'Don't be like that.'

'No. I love you too.' I give in and cling to her again and she clings back and it feels unnatural, wrong, to break away, not least because I know that when she comes back she'll be full up with family feeling and guilt, and this part of her life will be buried under it.

This isn't goodbye for a fortnight, this is goodbye to the loving part of Juliette for a lot longer than that. It makes me cling to her, think about her, far more than if I could trust her always to be the same – positively laboratory conditions for fostering addiction.

We move slowly, burdened by suitcases, to the front door. I wave her off into an afternoon that's sparkling with frost. The streets are grey under their patchy blanket, the air chill with the promise of snow. I watch as she gets into an enemy taxi, slams the door, smiles and is gone.

I go aching back into the sitting-room, look around it. The

lights from the Christmas tree are shining softly. I gaze at it, and at the single large present under it, its label saying 'to dearest Miranda, from Jay'. I've got two days to decide if I want to go to Bedford, or to stay here. Bleak desert either way. So much emptiness here, I think despairingly, can I bear it?

I switch on the TV – some inane thing. A fortnight of this looms before me. I pick up the remote, fling it as hard as I can against the wall: 'It's not fair, God, it's just not fucking fair...' I howl, to whoever may be listening. 'I'm sick of always being on my own – *sick of it.*'

God, about as present as Juliette, doesn't answer. It's only me, in this hollow, echoing cave. Alone, to sink or swim as I may.

Just as I'm wondering if suicide really isn't the answer, and how to do it -- hang myself in tinsel, electrocute myself with the fairy lights, and why don't I have a gun – there is a knock at the door.

I lever myself off the couch, squash the flying, desperate hope that it's Jay and go to the door. It's Ross. He's looking very festive, and he's also rather drunk.

'Darling Miranda! Happy Christmas!' he beams defiantly, waving a bottle of champagne.

He can come in.

'Where's Robert?' I ask, going into the kitchen for glasses.

'At his works Christmas party. And why am I not there, you may ask, with my beloved?' he queries, as if it's a riddle.

'You don't like office parties?' I say, entering into the spirit.

'I adore them.'

'Perhaps you dislike turkey, crackers, drunken revellers?'

'Indeed not. Drunken revellers in particular I am very fond of.' Ross tries to leer.

'Could it be that you are scared of going out after dark?' I venture, pouring the champagne.

'After dark is when all the best things happen.'

I hand him a glass of champagne. We're like two Cinderellas who never got to the ball.

'You didn't get invited, did you?'

'Indeed, I did not,' he hisses, 'and it is their loss, their sad and sorry, pitiful loss.'

I raise a glass. 'Welcome to the ranks of the dispossessed, my friend.'

'Cheers.' He drinks deeply, holds out the glass for a refill. Gathers bravado. 'You know, I wouldn't mind so much if only he'd come clean about why he's doing it, but no. It's all, "It's for my career's sake, pushkin, I'll never get a partnership if they find out," when the truth is, he's just scared.' Ross drains his glass again. 'Scared of being the office nancy boy, scared of all the shit he'd have to take.'

'You can't blame him for that.'

'I don't,' Ross sighs. 'I blame him for dressing it up, for not being honest with me.'

'Yeah,' I say, obsessed with my own problems, 'He's out to his family, though.'

'That's true.' He looks at me shrewdly, refills both of our glasses. 'It's just a nightmare going out with someone who isn't.'

I feel an almost sensual relaxation at the prospect of *talking* about it. I'm not out at work, everybody there thinks I'm a sad act who, at thirty, lives with her female friend. Not even in American sitcoms is that considered a good option.

I drink deeply. 'It's stupid... it seems to take over everything. It's like, until she has the guts to tell them, "Yes, I'm gay and no, it's not disgusting," she can't believe it herself.'

There is a pause. We stare, gloomily ashamed, into our glasses, thinking of all the times we've let bigotry stand and said nothing.

'If you don't fight prejudice, you end up believing it,' Ross finally murmurs.

'I think it's the other way around. She won't fight it because she believes it... and she can't bear her family to know how disgusting she is. She really does believe that she is disgusting, that this is disgusting, yet she also knows how lovely and sweet and... pure it is, how about love. She wants to share that with her parents, yet she's scared that if she does she'll lose them. She's going round in a tailspin, and the relationship's just going round with her.' I sigh and lie flat on the carpet. Ross looks down at me solemnly.

'Until she loses them,' he intones, and I know that what he's going to say will be the truth, 'she's never going to properly be an adult. When people keep us hanging on by a thread like that, not letting us be ourselves, they just keep us dependent children. It's a terrible thing to do, make your child think you'll stop loving her if she's this, that or the other, and it leaves it only two choices – to be itself and tell them to get stuffed, or –'

'– do what Jay's doing.'

'She's going to lose you, if she's not careful...'

'Oh, I don't know. I'm in it too deep.' We both jump as the telephone rings. My heart does its usual leap, *'It's Jay.'* My body lunges for the receiver before I've realised what it's doing. 'Hello?'

It's Jay. My side of the call is: 'Happy Christmas... how's it going? Good... I miss you... yes, I know you can't talk. Do you miss me too? Good... look, could you talk to me like I actually mean something to you? Yes, I *know* your family's all around you – actually, talking to me like you don't really know me is probably more of a give-away than you realise... Well, would you talk to your other friends like this? Exactly. Jay, either talk to me as though you love me, or just go away... Right, fuck off then.' I put the phone down sadly. *'Honestly!'*

'Family all around?' Ross asks flatly.

I gulp champagne. 'Oh yes – she was like a cross between a robot and a POW... "HelloMirandaHowAre*You*." God, it's pathetic. Shit! Do you ever imagine, Ross, what it would be like if "homosexuality" had never been condemned... if we were able to just be completely open about it?'

'Heaven,' he says extravagantly.

'Yeah, it would be...' I pause, thinking. 'D'you know what I miss? I miss not being able to hold hands in public, or to kiss. We went to Regent's Park and there were a few straight couples lying on top of each other, practically having full-blown bloody sex. Jay and I lay side by side and held hands, but I was so scared someone would see us, it took all the fun out of it.'

'It's an unequal world, all right. All you can do is make it as equal as you can in your own circle.'

We pause. The Christmas tree twinkles down on us. Outside a few happy people laugh, slither home in the frost.

'Yeah, well,' I raise my glass. 'Happy Christmas, neighbour...'

'I went out with a total closet case, once... no fun.'

'No,' I agree drunkenly.

'No birthdays together...'

'No Christmases, or New Years.'

'No being accepted by the family.'

'The "*family*",' I toast, and we drink to them solemnly.

'No one-bedroom flat.' Ross throws his hands up in horror at the idea.

'Self-loathing and disgust – if your parents are arseholes like Jay's.'

Then we move onto the more general Joys of being Gay.

'Queer-bashing...'

'The Church...'

'Always one to be thankful for.' Solemnly, we clink glasses, drink.

'Hypocrisy – no connection, of course.'

'No legal marriage...'

'No *children*,' I intone.

'Ah, that's changed...'

'That's true.' I raise my glass to it.

'Better representation in the media... the odd role model for the kiddies.'

I think. 'Stephen Fry.'

'Bless him... Sandi Toksvig...'

'Dale Winton?'

'We'll see...'

We think, come up with no one else. 'Yes, it is a little list, isn't it?' Ross sighs sadly.

And so we move on.

'Being able to foster...'

'And adopt...'

'Not being sent to prison any more... that's got to be good.'

'Never my problem,' I say smugly, and Ross raises his glass ironically, to me and every other lesbian.

'Do you think it's true, about Queen Victoria just not believing it happened?'

'Oh yes,' says Ross definitely.

'Stupid great married tart... bloody Victorian hypocrisy... I've got another bottle in the fridge, let's have it.' I stumble off. When I return, Ross is looking pensive.

'It's probably more that what happened between women was seen as not important... a little dabbling, something for the girls...'

I pop the cork, pour. Bubbles fizz. 'I alwaysh wondered why it hadn't gone the other way,' I slur. 'You know, male chauvinism and all that... why it didn't occurred to them that it was the "manly" option to be with other men and cut women out completely... like the ancient Greeks.'

'Ah yes, a woman for duty, a boy for pleasure –'

'– and a goat for ecstasy,' we finish together, and collapse in alcoholic hysterics. It's bloody good.

'Well, I wouldn't know about that,' Ross gasps, flicking champagne at me as I arch an eyebrow, 'but the reason it never became the "manly" option is because they saw faggots as taking the woman's role – and who wants that?'

'Aha,' I gloat, 'I knew mis... mis... *woman-hating*... was in there somewhere.'

We are now both completely pissed.

'Oh, I've got a good one.' Ross imitates a bigoted straight: 'I've got nothing *against* them, Mavis, it just seems so sad. None of their relationships seem to *last*, do they? It's such a lonely life...'

'To ire – irony,' I raise my glass.

'Glad to be Gay.'

'I-yi've got to go... somewhere.' I struggle to my feet with difficulty, stagger to the loo, rush back, tripping over the mat, 'Ooops, bloody thing.' I kick it, fall back down. 'Actually, I *am* glad to be gay... especially when I see how much shit straight women have to put up with.'

'Ye-ess...?'

'I just don't trust men, that's all. I'm always amazed at women who do. I used to think,' I snigger, 'that straight women were just *braver* than me, but then I realised –' I gesture wildly, arms windmilling to show the hugeness of the discovery, leaning in to stare solemnly right at Ross '– it's for real... they really *do* trust those bastards. I mean, I like straight men, some of my best friends are straight white men, aha...'

'Aha,' Ross echoes sourly.

'I just... there's so much pressure that seems to go with it... got to be thin, got to be smooth, got to look up to them still, just that *little bit*.' I pinch my thumb and middle finger together, squint at them as they waver as if they're underwater. I blink, continue, 'I've seen women pulling in eighty grand a year to their husband's thirty-five, still doing most of the child-care and housework – and still getting stick for not doing it properly – when it's only thirty years ago men were revered for going out to work, and it was considered despicable if they were asked to do anything in the evening to help at all.'

'Ah, halcyon days...'

'Well, not for you,' I say tartly.

'True. I'd have been asking strangers if they were a friend of Dorothy and shaking their hand in funny ways.'

I take a furious, drunken slug of champagne. 'The whole thing just makes me so angry... it's so bloody *illogical*.'

'Not from the male point of view,' Ross points out, reasonably enough.

'Oh, come on... somewhere deep down you've all got to know it's unfair. That's probably why you treat women so badly – angry for feeling guilty.'

'Not these days... everything's genetic these days... we can't even iron...'

'Do *not* get me started on that.'

'Me either!' Ross looks down indignantly at his beautifully ironed shirt and trousers, and probably loafers, too, for all I know. I never iron anything if it can be avoided, something else about me that drives Jay crazy. Ha-ha, I cackle drunkenly to myself, then think of us, then think of what makes me relax the most with it.

'The *equality* of a gay relationship is such a turn-on... such closeness. There just isn't that in a straight relationship.'

'How would you know?'

'True,' I agree, with all due apologies to Armistead Maupin, 'their ways *are* a mystery to me, but I'm sure they don't call it the war of the sexes for nothing.'

'Equality within the relationship, or equality with the rest of the world... island or mainland?'

'All is paradox.'

'Are you sure that what you've got with Jay is equality?'

My drunken omnipotence is shaken. 'What?'

Ross takes a deep breath. 'Look –' and at that moment we hear a knock on the door and Robbie's voice saying, *'Ross, it's me. Please come upstairs. I'm sorry, I'm so sorry, come out and talk to me NOW.'*

Ross sighs shakily, says with massive drunken wisdom, 'Ah, that'll be *Robert*... Look –' he bends down and kisses me '– take care of yourself, yes? And come and spend some of Christmas Day with us.'

Oh, Robert'll be delighted. 'I'll see... thanks.'

'No, we'd like to have you.'

'Thanks.' How did I end up in this position – a charity case for the neighbours? Surely it's only *old* ladies who end up being taken in on Christmas Day and I'm not even thirty yet. Oh, I should have *done* something, should have arranged something, but all I want to do is be with Jay.

'See you later, then,' carols Ross, and he rushes off to love and Robbie.

After ten minutes, the sitting-room seems very lonely without him. I turn on the little lamp, stare at the Christmas tree, think of what Jay'll be doing right now. No point wondering if she'll be thinking of me – I know she won't. She'll have too many other things to do, family things to do. I switch on the television, hear a choir singing 'Silent Night'.

I reach drunkenly for my glass, toast the empty air and the choir, and Jay, wherever she may be, whatever she may be doing. 'Merry Christmas.'

Part Two

Twelve

Jay came back after Christmas as cold and withdrawn as I knew she would and it didn't pass over. Nothing was right: the flat, me, work, nothing. I went to work in the mornings rigid with tension from yet another row and came home rigid with the dread of what I'd find. Work itself offered the odd moment of forgetting, but that was all.

The days flowed into a pattern: I left the house earlier and earlier to avoid her, getting more and more tired, until I could hardly drag my feet along the road. Mornings and evenings, I remember treading the same path on the same pavement, stomach churning, the world swirling around me, the huge expanded love I felt for her shrinking to a ball inside me, until it got so tiny I felt that one day I'd just be able to excrete it right out of me.

I got crabbier and crabbier with the outside world. The relationship took up every ounce of energy I had. If I turned my back on her for a second, let my energy flag, it wasn't safe. The pleasure of friends or outings wasn't worth the misery of later – of violence or the emotional deep freeze. Making sure Jay was happy was becoming my world and I lied to my friends about why I couldn't see them. I even resented their kindness. The strain had to come out somewhere and I nearly came to blows with one woman who pushed in front of me at the supermarket till.

The violence from Jay got worse, until I became scared to say anything at all, could hardly remember what it was like not to be half afraid of her always. I became placatory and more and more resentful, angry at myself for not being braver; and furious with her for doing this to me. Sex stopped altogether: my defences were up completely and I felt nothing when she tried. I was abasing myself enough as it was without bringing the person who wouldn't love me to climax.

I don't know how I didn't get an ulcer during those months, as winter turned to spring, but eventually, when the rows and the atmospheres were more frequent than the reconciliations, I said what I never thought I'd say. I said I'd leave her, if things didn't improve. And the only way things would ever get any better, I yelled, was if she got the guts from somewhere to tell her parents about us. Because her guilt and shame were corroding us and ruining us and what was more important to her, anyway? 'Push,' I screamed, in true Hollywood fashion, 'has come to shove, Juliette, *this is it*.'

*

Result: it is now Easter and her parents, who think they are spending the break with their little girl and her flatmate, are in for the shock of their lives. *If* she can do it. And oh, how I hope she can. I see a new life for both of us opening up, once the deceit is gone.

'It's not as easy as all that,' Jay whispers frantically to me now, eyes swivelling. Nora and Jim are in the bedroom.

'Either you do it or I – Hello! Did you sleep well?'

'Yes, thanks,' smiles Nora. 'And what are you two whispering about?'

'Oh, this and that.' Now that it's actually happening, my stomach has that fallen-down-a-lift-shaft feeling, so heaven only knows what Juliette's going through.

'Well,' beams Jim, 'what are we going to do today?'

Oh, have a heart attack?

'I think that Jay would like to have a little talk with you both,' I say quickly, before she or I bottle out.

Nora looks mildly bewildered. 'Really, dear, what about?' Today she's wearing a Littlewoods lacy cardy, silky top and icky skirt. Still looks respectable as ever, but there's nothing respectable about terrifying your own child.

'About... about... can I tell you later, Mam?' Jay glares at me.

'Of course, darling. You know we're always here for you.' Platitudes are about to be tested, I think, feeling sicker than ever.

'I hope that's true,' Jay whispers. I squeeze her arm comfortingly and Nora gives me a funny look. Maternal instinct not quite defunct in you, then, I think, giving her a sickly smile.

'Right, well, let's go if we're going,' Jim cuts in, all manly impatience, and we dutifully file out for our Easter lunch.

Later that evening, we're back at the starting post.

'Do it now,' I hiss.

Jay is sheet white and shaking like a leaf. 'I can't...' Sweat gleams on her upper lip, plasters her hair in strands to her brow.

'Yes, you can,' I whisper fiercely. 'We agreed – it's got to be done.' I feel like Lady Macbeth. Hopefully, we'll have a happier outcome.

'OK. All right, I'll do it... but in my own time.' Terrified of jumping overboard, more scared still of being pushed.

Jim and Nora come in.

'Right. So, Juliette, what's this major thing that you've got to tell us?'

We all take deep breaths.

'Mam, Dad,' Jay starts, then, losing confidence, 'would anyone like a drink?'

No one would. Get on with it, we're all screaming silently, as the suspense mounts.

'OK, right, well, this isn't easy for me to say, and I – I really hope that once I've –' she swallows '– once I've told you, it won't be as bad as I think it's going to be.'

'Dear God...' Nora is now as grey and shaking as her daughter. 'Are you trying to tell us you've got cancer?'

Lovely, lovely. Maybe that'll soften her up for later – well, for any minute now. I'm shaking so violently that I have to sit down.

'No, no, I'm fine. In fact, I'm very happy – or I could be, if you'd only –'

'*What is it?*' howls Jim.

'I've met someone I really like, who makes me very happy,' she gabbles and, despite myself, I preen.

'But that's great,' Jim says, bewildered.

'Oh darling,' says Nora emotionally and tries to hug Jay, who won't let her.

'We were starting to wonder if you ever would,' says Jim, tactful as always, and then, through the clouds of joy, they realise something's still not right.

'So when can we meet him?' he demands, every inch the concerned father, ready to beat 'him' to a pulp should 'he' not be good enough. Let's hope that his old-fashioned ideas extend, unlike his daughter's, to a refusal to attack women.

'Well, that's the thing, Dad,' stutters Jay. 'You see – the thing is –' I silently urge her on, as though she is a horse I have a huge bet on coming up to the winning-post.

'– The thing is –' Jay carries on, though she is now greenish-white with terror '– the thing is...' And then she falters at the very edge of the cliff. 'I can't tell you this, I'm sorry.' She looks at me.

'Oh darling,' Nora is all maternal concern and understanding, 'is he married?'

'No-o-o.'

'So what's the problem?' Clearly Jim feels that bluntness will get to the truth, the way it did when she was small.

'Right.' Jay steadies herself for the plunge once more. 'Well, it's not a problem... well, only inasmuch as you might think so... you see –' and again she puts a foot out over the abyss '– actually, I'm not exactly everything you I think I am.' Then, like a little girl scared of her own daring, she retreats hastily if temporarily back to solid parental land. 'Oh, please don't shut me out of your lives after I've told you this.'

'Darling, we love you, you're our daughter, please, just tell us.' Nora's voice is strained.

'Your mother's right, sweetheart, whatever it is, we're here for you. Now come on, tell us what the problem is.'

'I-I'm not sure I can, actually.'

'Jay, we didn't bring you up to be a coward.'

'No, but you did bring me up to hate certain things...'

'Yes, so? That was part of our job as your parents,' states Nora, aware as ever of the vast complexities of human existence.

'Yes, but... what if one of the things you hate is actually... connected with me?'

'Honey,' says Jim, by now convinced that she's murdered someone, 'whatever you've done, we'll stand by you.'

'Of course we will, but please, just tell us... Jay?'

The tension is so thick it's almost palpable. Jay looks unable to believe that it's come to this, that she is doing this.

People who've been bungee jumping talk of having to push themselves against their every instinct to leap into space. That's certainly how Jay's feeling now. I hover protectively, want to put my arms around her.

She gulps. 'Right. OK. Well, you know Miranda...'

To my horror they both look at me. I feel like an insect under a microscope and go scarlet.

'Ye-e-s,' says Nora cautiously.

'Well, you know how fond I am of her...'

'Yes, we do, we both do,' Jim almost snaps, in his impatience to get to the heart of the matter.

Pause. There should be a drum-roll for this moment, as the tension gathers, ready to snap. The storm is almost upon us.

'Well, it's – it's a bit more than –' and she falters, unable to go on. No matter, they understand. The storm's here.

Jim gives her a revolted look. 'Are you trying to tell us that you're – that you and Miranda are – are *together*?'

And I think of Bill and of how he kept his possible shock and disappointment to himself and only gravely said, 'Well, I can't say I approve, but –'

'Oh God no, you're not, are you, Juliette?' Nora screeches, suddenly every inch the outraged Catholic. 'No, you can't be.'

And I think of Katherine and how at least she didn't scream at me. Admittedly, what she did do was to keep saying, 'It's only a phase. You're not really one of *them*,' but there was none of this venom, none of these histrionics. In retrospect, it seems very civilised, very grown-up and beautifully controlled. On the other hand, maybe they sensed that I genuinely didn't care if they banished me, and so I had all the power. Juliette's parents know all too well how much power they have here, now, in this room.

'Dear God, girl,' bellows Jim, 'after everything we've taught you, are you seriously telling us that you're one of "them"?'

A pause that only lasts a moment, but seems to go on forever, fills the room. We're at a crossroads, destined to go down one path or the other in the next few seconds. Which path is it going to be?

'Oh please,' I beg silently, 'please.' I stare at her with all the longing of the best of our relationship in my eyes.

Jim and Nora are looking at her with all the loathing she has dreaded for so long showing clearly in theirs.

'How could you do this to your mother?' I hear Jim bellow from a great distance. Also from that distance, I hear Nora weeping, and...

'*No!*' cries Jay, a great exclamation of denial dropping into the silence. A path closes off, and time jolts up again.

'What?' barks Jim.

'No. No, I'm not gay... what on earth made you think that?'

And we're back to the utter mundanity of lies.

'Well, the way you were talking... so you've got a boyfriend?'

'Yes!'

What?

Predictable outpouring of joy.

'Oh darling, that's wonderful news... and is it serious?'

'... Yes.'

'Oh, darling, I'm so happy for you. Isn't that great, Jim?'

All else has been eclipsed for Nora; Jim isn't quite so easily put off the scent. 'Yes, it certainly is, but then –?'

'Oh, wait till I tell Sinead... So, what's his name?'

We all look expectantly at Jay, who stares wide-eyed back at us.

'... Martin?'

'Martin!'

'So what was it that you had to tell us about you and Miranda? Have you two had some sort of a fight?'

'No,' I say quietly, sick to my stomach with disappointment.

Jay glances nervously at me, knowing she's in trouble. 'Not yet!' she mutters. 'No, it was –'

'Oh, sweetheart, are you – are you – you know – pregnant?'

'No! No, it's... nothing, really... I was probably just worried about how you'd react about... Martin.'

'Silly girl,' cries Nora, giving her a hug.

'Yes,' says Jim, stroking his double chin thoughtfully. 'Oh, come here!' and he holds out his arms.

Jay goes into them like a homing pigeon.

'You'll always be my girl, you know that.'

I want to vomit. Two minutes ago, when he thought she was a lesbian, he was readying himself to chuck her away. Now, because of 'Martin', she'll always *'be his girl'*.

Sooner her than me, really.

'So when can we meet him?'

Get out of that one, Jay.

'A-ha,' she stalls nervously, as well she might. 'Well... well, he doesn't come here often.'

For some reason, Jim shoots me a hostile look.

'And why not?' he asks softly.

'Well... it's handier at his place,' Jay explains, and again Jim puts her embarrassment down to something else and scowls at me.

'Is it now?' he says, 'and why would that be?'

'Does it matter, Jim?' Nora, still on Cloud Nine, is determined to stay there. 'Why make such a big deal about it? Couples usually prefer to stay at one place rather than another.'

'Aye, and there's usually a reason for it.'

'Well, whatever it is, I'm sure it's not important.'

'No, that's right, Dad,' interjects Jay nervously.

'Jay, what were you going to tell us before? About you and *Miranda*?'

'What? Oh, nothing...'

'So you're not going to tell us? Well, I think I've guessed, and I think we should talk about it more *tomorrow*.' Family Only, says his tone.

I've had enough. 'That's OK, you can talk about it now,' I snap. 'I'm going out.'

'Where to?' Jay demands.

I shrug, get my coat, and make good my escape.

'Goodnight, dear,' calls Nora cosily. That woman! She's like the Larson cartoon of Satan's Mam, who insists on serving cookies and milk to the damned, ignoring all the evidence that this isn't Suburbia.

'See you later?' Jay asks tentatively.

I walk out and, before the door shuts behind me, I hear Jim growl, 'I think you should move out of here, Juliette.'

Ross and Robbie are out, so I spend a couple of hours just walking. When I get back, chilled to the bone, I hear Jay call softly, 'Is that you?'

'Well, it isn't Martin.' I push open the sitting-room door and go in. The sofa-bed and the little truckle bed are made up and only the lamp is on, casting a rosy glow over Jay, who is sitting cross-legged on the sofa-bed in red tartan pyjamas, as enticing a picture of domestic cosiness as you could ever hope to come across. Only it is not my cosy harmony, it's hers and her parents'.

She looks up at me as I stalk around, dropping my coat, ripping off my jumper.

'I'm sorry.'

'Sure you are.'

'I am sorry... I'm so sorry... I just can't tell them.'

I sit down on the truckle bed. 'Not now?

'Not ever.'

And there it is. Flat acceptance of the fact that Family comes First.

'Ri–' To my surprise, I start to cry. 'Right.'

Jay untangles herself and comes and sits beside me. For once, I've got her full attention.

'Oh, don't... please don't.' She puts her arm around me, pulls me close. I smell jasmine soap, Natrel and Jay. Oh *God*, I want her for my own. I sigh, try to pull myself together.

'I'm sorry. I'm being silly... it was just when I thought you were going to tell them... I was so excited. Sick for you, of course, but excited. I just felt so... so... wa-ha-nted...' and I break down completely.

'I know,' she says, grief in every syllable, 'I'm sorry...' and she holds me to her, gently kisses the side of my head. 'Come into bed with me.'

I shake my head. 'I can't. You know I can't... what if one of them comes in?'

'I don't care... come in.'

We climb into the big bed and lie down wearily, my head on her breast. I feel the comfort of her warm, breathing body. Time passes.

'This is nice...' I say, finally relaxing, and just then we hear footsteps in the hall. Jay suddenly moves with the speed of cheetah, and is safely back in 'her' bed, the covers bundled over her head, when the door opens a second later, letting in a shaft of light that reveals Jim standing there, in his pyjamas.

'Everything all right, girls?' he asks, with the air of a watchful nursery nurse.

While I seethe at his nerve, Jay says, 'Yes, thanks, Dad. Go back to bed.'

He pauses for a moment, then agrees: 'Aye, OK. Night, then, Jay.'

'Night, Dad.'

The door closes behind him, swallowing us up in the blackness left behind. After a moment, Jay's voice squeaks up, 'I don't think we'd better risk it again.'

'Fine,' I say tersely.

'Night night, then.' I don't reply. 'Goodnight. Miranda? Night, then.'

As she composes herself for sleep, I am left fuming, and rehearsing the many things that could have been said tonight – not least to Jim just now.

Thirteen

This time, the goodbyes are excruciating. Jim is still hostile, and for some reason Nora is finding it impossible to look at me. We all hover in the sitting-room while they fuss over multitudinous bags. Finally, Nora looks up, ready to go.

'Right, well, bye Jay, you take care now,' she says emotionally, hugging and kissing her daughter as though Jay's about to set sail on the *Mayflower*.

'I will,' she says stoically back, 'bye, Mam...'

'And tell Martin from us that we can't wait to meet him.' Jay looks awkward. 'OK?' Nora insists. This Martin thing's not going to be allowed to be dropped.

Jay, examining her nails closely, manages to mutter, 'OK.'

Nora, satisfied, picks up her bags and heads for the door. Once she's reached it, she clearly thinks it's safe to turn and – finally – look at me.

'Goodbye, then, Miranda,' she says in a strangled voice.

'Bye, Nora, take care,' I say, my voice implying that I don't give a shit if you do or if you don't or if Jim shoves you out of the car onto the motorway.

'Aye, you too,' she says quickly, and with the same amount of warmth as me, then, her voice changing back to Loving Mammy, 'Speak to you soon, Jay.'

'Yeah.' Jay is glad, so glad, that they're going, but also that they're going with relationships intact.

Nora buggers off to the car. Now there's only Jim to be got through. He's been pottering in some corner, biding his time like a sodding great spider.

'Bye then, lass,' he says, arms open wide to engulf his daughter. 'Great news about Martin...'

'Yeah.' She's going to have to start saying that with more enthusiasm, or they're going to twig. Then again, maybe not. Jim gives her an extra squeeze, picks up his suitcase and heads for the door, clearly with no intention of saying anything to me. Butterflies start up in my stomach.

'Bye, Jim,' I trill, feeling cheeky for even daring it.

'Goodbye Miranda,' he says coldly, as though he's talking to an impudent servant.

'Now remember what I said to you,' he adds to Jay, with all the gravitas of a Victorian patriarch.

'No, I won't, because it's ridiculous,' she says firmly.

What? What? What is ridiculous? What is going on here? What has been going on behind my back?

'Aye, well, we'll see.' And Jim is gone too. We wait in frozen silence till their car starts up, then release ourselves back into life. I turn on her. 'What did he say to you?'

'Oh, nothing we need to worry about.'

'*What?*'

'They've worked out that you're gay,' Jay says flatly. 'They now think that you're a bad influence on me and they want me to move out.'

I feel as if I've been hit in the stomach by a two-by-four plank of wood. I remember Bill and that familiar feeling, that I'm not worthy of being treated with respect, that whatever I do, however I try to fit in, it all just slips away from me in the end and I'm left alone, sidelined in my little box, while they all get on with the business of loving each other. And that's the moment I decide, sod them all, Bill and Katherine, Nora and Jim, I'm just not going to bother any more. If Katherine and Bill can leave me at the mercy of forever having to find parental figures, then sod them, and Nora and Jim are simply beyond contempt.

I pull myself together enough to say, in a voice that doesn't sound like mine, 'And are you going to?'

Jay is clearly taken aback. 'That's a very stupid question. I assume it was meant to be a joke?'

'I don't know... you thought telling your parents about an imaginary boyfriend was a sensible idea. We have different ideas about what's funny.'

'What was I meant to do?' she demands.

'What? You were *meant* to tell them that you're gay! You were *meant* to tell them that I'm the woman that you love, that we've been together over six years! You were *meant* to tell them the truth.'

'I know...' she says sheepishly

'So what's going to happen when they want to meet "Martin"?'

'I don't know.'

'I think this is going to end with your moving out, d'you know that? They'll keep going on and on at you about how you shouldn't be living with a lesbian, about how bad it is in the eyes of the Lord. *Then* they'll start in with the suspicious looks and phrases again: "unless you *like* living with her", "unless there's more to this than meets the eye", "is there something you'd like to tell us?"'

'If only they would say that,' she sighs wistfully.

'You'd probably end up saying you and Martin are getting married,' I scream.

'Don't be ridiculous.'

'Yes... when you're introducing some stranger to them as "Martin, my intended" and they're falling all over themselves to kiss his ass, I'll tell myself that *I'm* the ridiculous one.' I take a couple of deep breaths, then have to ask, 'What are you going to do?'

'I don't know.'

Frustrated beyond belief, I march to the cupboard where the gay things are hiding. 'At least these can come back out now.' And I shove the posters up, lay out the books and ornaments, reverentially take out the photo.

I may not be able to get my lover to tell her parents about me, I may not be able to get these parents to like me now they know I'm a lesbian, I may not be able to have my flat decorated the way I want while they're here, but by God, now they've gone, those decorations are going back up if it kills me.

Fourteen

Three weeks later, we're cuddled up on the sofa, watching *Claire of the Moon*. Sex is definitely on the menu for later: the vibrator is out and waiting, along with the strap-on dildo and a huge bottle of Sensual massage oil. Light is coming from a candle in the shape of two women kissing – I sent off for it from the PG World catalogue. Above the sofa is a huge new poster of two naked women twined around each other; the photo of us kissing is now slap-bang in the middle of the mantelpiece and a rainbow throw decorates the sofa-bed.

I may have gone slightly too far. But it's nice, and it's definitely getting us in the mood. I sigh languorously, stretch like a cat in anticipation of what's coming.

Jay smiles at me, slips her hand caressingly inside my shirt. I squirm. This is going to be a long evening.

Just then, the doorbell rings. I press myself lazily back into the couch.

'I'll go,' sighs Jay.

'Oh good.'

I lie back, run my hand down my stomach, back up, cup my breasts, finger the nipples, expecting Jay to get rid of whatever casual caller this is.

'Mam! Hi! Oh my God!'

I leap round like a mountain goat on the crags, ripping down posters, shoving books and ornaments away. I slam the TV off, rip the throw off the sofa. It swirls around me like a multi-coloured parachute. I do a little dance on the carpet, bundling and *bundling* its many folds, wondering frantically where to put it. In the end, I peer furtively out the door, then, with some of it trailing behind me like a rainbow train, I nip into the kitchen with it, look wildly round and shove it hysterically into the oven.

Rushing back to the sitting-room, I violently thrust videos and their boxes into the cabinet. The strap-on also gets dumped in there. The photo I slide regretfully into a drawer, giving it a quick pat before slamming the drawer shut and looking wildly round the room.

'*Sinead too*! This *is* a surprise! What are you doing here? Aha – *why are you here*? Yes, of course you can come in.'

I grab the vibrator, wrestle it into one of the tiny top drawers of the oak chest. I slam the drawer shut, grab the bottle of oil – and the damn vibrator has clicked on! It's buzzing through the wood, I want to scream, 'It's *buzzing*... through the wood!' I jump

– 'Aargh!' – and drop the bottle, which shatters, and the smell of sandalwood and musk spreads through the flat. '*Aargh*!'

Footsteps tramp through the hall and they're upon me. I look up, too flustered to be nervous.

'Hi!'

'Hi,' says Nora, with no warmth whatsoever. In the following silence, we all look at the drawer. It sounds as though a swarm of bees is in it. To my feverish imagination, it seems the vibrator is jerking the whole chest sideways. Nora and Sinead look at it with raised eyebrows. Jay looks faint.

'What's the matter with your drawer?' Sinead finally inquires, breaking the spell.

'It came from Ikea!' I say, banging it at what I hope is the right spot, as though I want to splinter the whole thing to matchsticks. 'This is a nice surprise –' I pant, beaming fixedly while leaning over the drawer and opening it a fraction, just enough to shove my hand in and finally turn the damn thing off. In the ringing silence that follows, I say lightly, 'So what brings you here?'

Nora blinks at me coldly. 'Yes, well, we were in London for a bit of shopping –' All the way from County Cork? '– and I suddenly thought: why not pop in and see Jay... and see if Martin's anywhere around, but –'

Imagining her disappointment to be scepticism, I leap in with, 'I think he's nipped out for some biscuits.' I am no good at thinking on my feet. Nora and Sinead stare at me as though I am mad.

'No,' Jay says through gritted teeth, 'How could he? He's in *Wolverhampton.*'

Embarrassed pause.

'So he is, I keep forgetting. Can I take your jackets?' I lunge forward manically and in doing so reveal the smashed bottle.

'That's what the smell was,' Sinead says brightly.

'Oh yes,' I beam, and grab the (nasty, cheap, black, imitation leather) jacket rather roughly from her. I then move towards Nora, who practically thrusts her C&A coat at me in a desperate attempt to stop me getting too close. No hugs and kisses this time.

'Sit down, Mam, Sinead... would you like a drink?'

'I'll have a small sherry, thanks, love.'

'I'd love a cup of tea,' says Sinead, every inch the Young Suburban Housewife.

'Great. I'll just go and –' Jay gestures kitchenwards, practically rubbing her hands together with forced bonhomie.

Sinead scampers after her, leering, 'I'll give you a hand. Then you can tell me all about *Martin.*'

'Oh good,' says Jay weakly, and they disappear into the kitchen.

Left alone with a Lesbian, Nora looks at me warily, as though I'm about to grow fangs and a forked tail and leap on her.

'So, how are you keeping, Miranda?' she asks at last.

'Couldn't be better.'

Pause while she assimilates this for hidden meanings. I don't ask about her.

'So... do you see much of Martin?' she says desperately, trying to get the conversation onto safe, straight ground. I chuck their coats carelessly down on the sofa, and sit down perilously close to them. Nora eyes me nervously.

'No. He's a difficult man to see much of.'

'Indeed. But I'm glad Jay's finally found someone.'

'Me too.' Conversation flags. I glance around warily. Hastily denuded of a lot of its decor, the sitting-room looks as forlorn as if we're in the process of moving out. Four little bits of Blu-Tack in four corners show where the poster was. Looking naked without the throw, the sofa-bed glares, gloomily green again and twice as depressing as before. And then I see the candle. Shit! In the mad rush, it got left where it was, and it's sitting, shining white, on a side table.

'We used to worry about her, you know,' Nora suddenly confides, leaning forward, as though to say, 'We used to worry that she was *like you*,' and why she is confident that I will understand, be sympathetic, I have no idea. The arrogance of the Moral Majority is beyond belief.

'I can imagine,' I say coldly.

Robbed of a confidante, Nora sits back for a beat, regrouping.

'So, do you think it's serious, this whole Martin thing?' she recovers enough to ask.

'Oh, I think it's a very serious situation indeed.'

Nora, ignoring my underlying tone, proceeds to enthuse about this, Irish accent growing stronger by the minute. 'Oh that's great. 'D'you think... could we possibly be hearing wedding bells in the near future?'

Oh. My. God. 'Well,' I say ironically, 'there is a wedding on in our local church tomorrow. If we go and stand outside the vestry at just the right moment, who knows?'

Nora doesn't know how to react to this. 'No, dear, I meant between Martin and Jay...'

'Is that what you want?'

'Well, if it's what she wants... but it would be lovely to see her get married, wouldn't it?' she prods, trying to head me in the right direction, make the handicapped be glad for her sweet friend who, in the best old film tradition, has found sweet normal happiness.

'Ye-es, I was just saying to Jay that I can certainly see it coming.'

Just then the Sisters re-enter, with a tray of drinks which Jay distributes. I've got white wine. I check Sinead hasn't spat in it while Jay's back was turned.

'Thanks, love,' says Nora, as composedly as if she's in her own sitting-room.

'Cheers,' I counter wryly.

Sinead and Jay sit down, Sinead pointedly moving the coats to a place of safety first.

There is an expectant pause.

'Well, this is a nice surprise,' says Jay, and I smile to myself, knowing her panties will be wet with anticipation of what we were going to do and that, while surprise this visit may be, nice it definitely is not. The flat is heavy with the scent of musk.

'We really did want to meet Martin this time,' Sinead pouts. 'We could all have had dinner together, just the *four* of us.' She glares at me. I glare back, taking her slightly by surprise.

'Ah, well...' Jay hedges, then stops, suddenly realising that she has no idea what to say next.

'So what are the *three* of you going to do?' I help her out.

'I don't know.' Sinead again. 'We might go out for dinner anyway. What d'you think, Juliette?'

'Yeah, sure, good idea.' Anything to get them out of the flat. 'Miranda, you'll come to?'

Is the woman mad? I'd rather spend the evening in a pool with some nice, honest piranha fish than spend it being eaten alive by these witches. Anyway, Nora soon enough makes it clear that I'm not invited: 'I'm sure Miranda's got... things of her own to do.' Delicate pause while she carefully doesn't think about what these things might be.

'Yeah,' agrees Sinead.

'Don't be ridiculous... Miranda, of course you'll come, won't you?'

Nora and Sinead glare at me in the most civilised way.

'Oh, I don't think so,' through the lump in my throat, 'but thanks...'

'Yeah, it wouldn't be quite your thing, would it, Miranda?' Sinead grinds out contemptuously.

'Why wouldn't it be, Sinead?'

'Well, you know,' she gloats, 'happy families, and all that. Wouldn't you prefer something a bit more... butch?'

'I don't know what you're talking about,' I say calmly, looking at Jay and Nora for any indication that they're going to stop her, but Nora is pointedly looking away, and Jay is shaking her head, indicating, 'don't rock the boat'.

'Oh, it's all right, Miranda, we know your little... secret now.'

'What? What little secret?' Let her say it.

'Well, that you're... you *know*... that way inclined.' She snickers at her own daring.

'You mean gay.'

'Yes, if you like.'

'Right. And obviously having the gay gene makes it impossible for me to enjoy intimate little family dinners. Actually, you know, you're right – that's exactly what it does do – with some families, anyway.'

'Miranda,' Jay says warningly.

'Oh, don't bother,' I snap, so angry and outraged that I can't show it properly, and it comes out as petulance, 'I'm going out. Enjoy your dinners!'

As I storm out, I hear Jay rebuke her little sister, 'Did you have to be so rude?' and Nora, damn her, say, 'You know, I think your father's right, Juliette... maybe you should consider moving out of here.'

I knew it. Why can't these people see that I'm not dangerous, that I only want to be loved?

I sneak home when the coast's clear, inviting Arabella round for back-up and to bring her up to speed. We get through a bottle of red wine and stick all the gay decorations back up. (Except the throw, which stays forgotten in the oven.) Again, the sitting-room glows.

Then Arabella looks round, and isn't as sure as I am that this is a good idea.

'Are you *shure* this is the way you want to go?' she asks, with beautiful, drunken, upper-class understatement.

'Why not? They know I'm gay *and* they've made it perftly clear that they don't approve – *in my flat* they've made it clear, so shod 'em. What'sh point of hiding any more?'

'Fair enough,' she slurs, almost as drunk as I am. 'So, Jay'sh got a boyfriend?' and she giggles.

'Only *Martin*!'

'Shit! Does he know?'

I start to laugh. I can't help it and it feels great to finally lighten up. 'Oh, Lordy Lord, the way things are going, I'm sure it's only a matter of time.'

'Pushkin's not going to be best pleased.'

'Then maybe him and me can get together... two straight couples for two gay ones. Won't the church be happy...'

'Yes. I must say –'

Just then we hear Jay crying, 'I'll go in and put the kettle on.'

'Goodbye then.' Arabella starts to get up. I can't say I blame her, but I'm not letting her go. I can't face them on my own again.

'Don't be so shilly.' I grab her back down. But, sadly, I'm starting to sober up.

Jay comes in.

'Hi, Arabella, hi hon,' she says casually, *en route* to the kitchen.

'Hi,' squeaks Arabella.

'Hello,' I say smugly.

'I was just going to –' Jay gestures kitchenwards, then catches sight of the decorations. 'What the hell?'

'What?'

'Why on earth did you –' and, panting like an animal in a trap, she starts to frantically take them down. I try to stop her.

'Do what? Live honestly?' I spit, grappling with her.

'Are you stupid or something?' She glares at me, frantically stuffing ornaments into her pockets. 'Do you know what they'll do if they see this?'

'Walk straight out again?' I suggest hopefully. 'Have a heart attack? Die? It's only –' I struggle with her as she tries to take down the new poster '– decorations, Jay.'

We each have an end of the poster when we finally hear Sinead and Nora walk in the front door. Jay panics, pulls the poster towards her, and it rips. We're left holding a naked woman each. Jay looks down at hers as if she can't believe her eyes and scrumples it up quickly as they walk in. She's actually managed to hide most of the stuff I put back out; only the ubiquitous candle remains. I eye it, but don't say anything.

'Right! I'll go and put the kettle on,' she squawks and exits like Basil Fawlty on speed.

Sinead is eyeing the remains of the poster. 'What's that?' she asks suspiciously.

'It *was* a poster.'

'Redecorating?'

'Constantly.'

Jay, fearful of something incriminating happening, rushes back in, grabs my half of the poster, and scrumples it up, too. 'Oh, it wasn't worth keeping,' she beams. '*Right*! I'll go and put that kettle on.'

That poster cost me twenty quid and I really liked it. 'Martin called for you,' I say, dropping the sentence like a stone down a well, stopping her in her tracks.

'Are you sure?'

Sinead and Nora are instantly agog.

'Of course I'm sure,' I coo sweetly. 'Why wouldn't your boyfriend phone here? Your family'll be thinking he's imaginary or something if you keep this up.' I laugh a tinkling laugh. Jay looks like she could happily murder me.

'What did he want?' she grits out, smiling for her family's benefit.

'To say he loves you, and he misses you –' Nora and Sinead say 'Aaaahh' here '– and he'll be home tomorrow.'

'What?' Jay yowls.

'Oh, that's so exciting... we'll finally get to meet him,' Sinead flaps.

'Yes, this is good news,' Nora says measuredly.

'How can he be coming home?' Jay gabbles. 'His course doesn't finish *till the end of next week*.'

'I think it finished early or something. Anyway,' I smile at the harpies, 'he's dying to meet you two.'

'Aaaahh...'

'He said he was sure you'd be thinking he was the invisible man or something... not having met you after all this time.'

'It hasn't been that long! Aha ha.'

'Maybe it just *feels* long to him, Jay.'

'No, he's not *that stupid*, Miranda.'

I smile at her relations. 'No, but it's only human nature to want to meet the in-laws, isn't it?'

'Absolutely,' agrees Nora.

'He sounds really sweet.'

Jay has one last stab at concealment: 'What time does his train get in? You may well be away by that time.'

'Don't be ridiculous, dear,' says Nora, scuppering that hope. 'We'll stay till midnight if necessary.'

I gleam evilly. 'Yes, they'll stay till midnight, if necessary... but it won't be. His train gets in at ten am, at Euston... and I told him you'd take the morning off to meet him.'

'Oohhh,' says Sinead, bang on cue, 'we could come too!'

'There you go... sorted.' I beam at Juliette. 'Why don't you go and put that kettle on now and we'll all have that nice cup of tea?'

Jay gulps, almost staggers, then takes a desperate grip on herself and the situation.

'Right. But I'll meet him on my own. A railway station's not the best place to meet someone for the first time.'

'Whatever you think best, dear,' murmurs Nora placidly, the Minotaur placated by the promise of fresh blood. 'So when *shall* we get to meet him?'

'What about tomorrow evening, when you've both finished work?' I suggest.

Juliette is beaten, and she knows it. 'Why not?'

'Oohh, lovely... tell you what, dear, why don't I make us all a nice supper?'

In *my* kitchen? 'Oh, feel free...'

Slightly embarrassed pause.

'Well, I *must* be going,' announces Arabella brightly, seizing the moment to get away before things turn really nasty, and she's halfway to the door before I register it. In truth, I'd forgotten all about her and genuine contrition bleeds through my rage.

'Oh, I'm sorry, how rude of us... Arabella, you haven't met Jay's mother and sister, have you? Nora and Sinead, this is Arabella.'

They come forward all smiles, ready to shake hands, until Jay says softly, 'Miranda's *special* friend,' and, as my head whips round to her in disbelief, the smiles freeze on their faces, and they step back a pace or two.

'How do you do?' says Nora stiffly.

'Hi,' waves Arabella nervously, suppressing hysteria.

'Hello,' says Sinead, looking her up and down.

There is a very awkward silence.

'Right, I'll be off then,' says Arabella desperately, and I leap forward to rescue her.

'OK, thanks for coming round...' and are you ever going to speak to me again?

'No, it was a... pleasure,' she attempts, struggling into her coat. 'So, I'll see you tomorrow, then.'

'Lovely... Actually –' I scowl at Jay '– if you're picking me up here, you'll probably get to meet Martin too.'

Sinead actually has the cheek to say, 'Oh, lucky Martin,' under her breath.

'OK, that'd be lovely.' Arabella backs toward the door.

'Great... I'll see you out then.'

'Oh, that's OK,' she says, hardly able to believe she's finally getting out of here. 'Right, then, bye, everyone.'

Jay and I are the only ones who respond and the door hasn't shut behind her before Nora is saying, 'So... what does Martin like to eat, Jay?'

I toy with the idea of jumping in and making him a vegan, but I can't be bothered. This has gone far enough.

'Oh, anything,' Jay says vaguely, 'I'll just go and...' She slopes off to the peace and sanity of the kitchen.

'All right, dear,' says Nora. 'This is so exciting, isn't it, Sinead?'

'Oh yes,' agrees the bitch, and, unable to resist having yet another jab at me, 'This must be quite sad for you, Miranda... never being able to have an occasion like this for yourself.'

I'm still slightly drunk. I stare at her thoughtfully. 'It's not very *cosy* in here, is it? I'll just light the candle for you, and then you can have a *good old* chin-wag.' I bend over, strike a match and the two entwined women leap into sharp focus.

'What a nice idea,' says Nora, not looking anywhere near it, 'Now, what if I do a roast?'

'I'll just switch off the main light...'

The candle burns bright. Jay, coming back in with a forced and determined smile and the tea-tray, nearly drops the tray in horror.

'Yeah, Mam,' witters Sinead, 'your roast lamb always goes down a treat.'

'I'll just –' squeaks Jay, sidling towards the light. Sinead and Nora swivel their terrible heads round in her direction and see the candle.

'Ah, tea, lovely,' says thick Sinead.

'What an unusual-looking candle,' murmurs Nora, getting up. 'Let's have a look at it – oh!'

Jay, with a turn of speed that would win her an Olympic gold in any tray-carrying competition, has got to it first, thrusting her mother aside. Drawing on all the remaining breath she has, she puffs it out. 'Miranda,' she gasps, desperately keeping the ball rolling (subtext 'I'm going to *kill* you'), 'what *are* you doing tonight? Keeping us all in the dark?' She laughs falsely. 'We don't need candles – Arabella's not here any more.' Casually, she stuffs the candle in her pocket, oblivious to the curious looks of her mother and sister, and yelps as she burns herself: 'Shit!' ... and Nora's other Roast Lamb is done. 'Tea, anyone? What's on TV tonight?'

'*La Cage aux Folles*,' I say sourly.

'No it isn't!' says Jay, panicked.

'It's on here all right.'

'I'll pour, shall I?' And that's Nora, bored with all this cryptic conversation.

'What's it about?' asks Sinead, interested.

'It's about two gay men who've lived together for donkey's years, and then their son tells them that he's getting married, and that his fiancée's parents are very right-wing. So the gay couple have to take all their *gay decorations* down –' I stare hard at Jay '– and pretend to be something they're not. It's really about all the mayhem that ensues.'

Nora, busily pouring the tea, says, 'Well, I don't think we want to watch that... Milk and sugar, Jay?'

'Please, Mam.'

'It doesn't even sound believable,' Sinead snorts, determined to pour vitriol on anything homosexual. She snorts, 'Get rid of all their gay decorations, indeed. What the hell are "gay decorations" anyway? D'you know, Jay?'

Jay, trying to sit down casually, is foiled by the candle. 'No idea, Sinead. I'll just go and dump this *candle*.' She glares at me as she passes, no doubt en route to the kitchen bin.

'Sinead, love, here's yours,' says the Chatelaine of the manor, handing out the tea-cups.

'Thanks, Mam.'

Slightly colder, 'Miranda?'

'No thanks, Nora.' Not even if I was dying of thirst in the desert, you old hag, would I take a drink from you now. Her head swivels again as her pet re-enters.

'So, dear,' she purrs, 'I imagine you're looking forward to tomorrow.'

Jay has the look of one who, having evaded the ambush, is taken by surprise by the ongoing war.

'Oh, immensely,' she rallies. 'Actually, I think I'll have a little brandy instead of tea tonight. Anyone else?'

We all decline. Jay pours herself a huge one.

'What do you think Martin would like for pudding?' Nora inquires casually.

Jay drains her brandy, reaches desperately for the bottle. 'Mam... I really have no idea at all.'

'Oh, that's all right, then, I'll do my apple and raspberry crumble.'

Gaahh!

That night, I sleep huddled under the throw. Jay covered it with a blanket, lest one of Them should come in during the night, but I've long since kicked that off.

Fifteen

Of course, Nora and Sinead sleep in our room that night. I am starting to hate that little truckle bed. Next morning, Jay is feverishly making plans to contain the chaos.

'Right,' she says, hopping on one leg, pulling her beautifully ironed beige trousers on, 'so I get a fax from Martin, saying he's really sorry, but he's got into all kinds of shit for even thinking about cutting this extremely important course short, and he's got to stay put. I then –' she zips her trousers, starts pulling on an immaculate cream blouse '– get extremely cross about this, and basically, this is the beginning of the end for poor old Martin and me. Right?' She tucks her blouse into her waistband, pulls it down neatly.

'I suppose so,' I say reluctantly.

'Well, don't sound so disappointed!'

'Oh, you deserve to be punished, you know.'

'Bullshit! For what?'

'For what, she says!'

'For trying to keep my parents loving me?'

'Oh please! That's not something –'

'I know, OK,' she snaps. 'Don't start all that again. It's just the way they are, and I can't change them.'

'So you're not even going to try?'

'No, I'm not – I mean, look at the way they're treating you!' She slips into her spotless coat.

'You mean, look at the way you're *letting* them treat me! Why are you letting them get away with all that? They're treating me like dirt and you're letting them. It's not exactly nice, being gay-bashed in my own home.'

Jay grabs her briefcase, is now ready for the off, her mind on work. 'I know, I know,' she says distractedly, 'it's not nice for me either, but it won't be for much longer. They'll be gone soon, and then things'll be back to normal.'

'Oh, lucky me.'

She comes over to kiss me. I back away.

'If that's the way you're going to be,' she says, 'I'm off to work.'

'Oh, give me a hug.'

'All right.' She comes towards me again, but just as she's close enough for me to smell her, yearn for her, we hear the bedroom door opening, and she jumps away. 'Right, so I'll see you tonight.'

'Yes,' I acquiesce wearily.

'Good,' she says softly, whispers, 'I love you... Get rid of the throw!'

'Yeah.' I attempt a grin. 'See you tonight.'

Juliette opens the door, looks through it nervously and blows me a kiss. I blow her one back.

'Bye.'

She walks into the hall, bumps into her mother. I hear, 'Morning, Mam.'

'Morning, darling. Sleep well, or were you too excited?'

Or were you too excited? *For fuck's sake*! I roll my eyes.

'No, I slept fine,' Jay is saying. 'Well, have a good day and I'll – we'll – see you tonight.'

'Sinead and I are really looking forward to it.'

'Me too. Bye, Mam.'

'Bye.' Nora comes straight into the sitting-room and looks at me in distaste, as though I'm an unwanted house guest.

'Morning, Miranda,' she says coldly.

'Nora... See you later.' Grabbing my coat and the throw, which is now in a bin-bag, I make a hasty exit.

'Oh... yes... you'll be here too, won't you?' she says dismally.

I leave before I strangle her, slamming the door. Let's wake Sinead up too. After delivering the throw to Ross ('Oh, lovely, a parachute!'), I glance in our window, see Nora fussily re-arranging the sitting-room and have to force myself to walk on, as I might otherwise go back in and tell her the truth there and then.

*

That evening, I sprawl in an armchair and watch, grinning.

'But I don't understand,' Sinead is wailing, 'I thought it was all arranged...'

'Well, obviously not well enough.' Jay is doing a pretty convincing impersonation of a woman scorned. 'Honestly, this is so like Martin. I'm tired of being let down by him. Once more, and I really think that's it over between us.'

'Ah,' coaxes Nora, 'you don't really mean that.'

'Oh, I *do*.'

'Ah, we'll see...'

'No, Mam, I really mean it... he's let me down once too often, the bastard.'

'Ah, I expect when you see him again it'll all be forgotten,' says Sinead.

'No, I don't think so,' says the little innocent, 'I'm probably better off on my own, here with Miranda.'

Sometimes I wonder how she manages to dress herself every morning. Does she really think that they are going to say, 'Oh, OK,' and relinquish her to the jaws of a Lesbian? Does she? Does she really? If she does, she is disappointed – Nora gasps out loud with horror and Sinead sucks in her breath with enough force to hoover in the entire sitting-room. With suction like that around, Owen is a very lucky man. Not that he deserves it, but hell, anyone who takes Sinead on needs every bonus he can get.

'Tea, anyone?' I offer blithely, and cannot believe their nerve when Nora says, 'Oh, yes, love.' The 'love' is sheer habit.

'Sinead, you'll have some too?'

'OK.'

'Juliette?' I ask.

She's still on a loop. 'No, thanks, Mir. Honestly, I feel so let down...'

'I'll get the tea then.' I go into the kitchen and eavesdrop shamelessly.

The second she thinks I'm out of earshot, Nora starts: 'I think there's something not quite right about this you and Miranda situation.'

'Tut, bloody men – what?'

'It's not healthy – you should want to be out with your boyfriend, not stuck in here with a... *lesbian*, meeting all her lesbian friends, with a couple of gay men above you.'

'Mam, I like it here and I like living with Miranda.'

'Why do you like it so much, though? What's the attraction?' Oh, be careful, Jay, be very careful here indeed. I press myself against the kitchen wall, next to the door, hold my breath. 'You don't even have a bedroom each...' I hear a slight suspicion dawning in her voice. 'Juliette, there *is* a Martin, isn't there?'

Sinead's voice next, bobbing about, interspersed with little thumps. I imagine she's wandering about the room, picking ornaments up, inspecting them carelessly, then dumping them down again, opening and shutting drawers. 'Oh, Mam, of course there's a Martin,' she whines. 'Don't be so silly – Jay's hardly going to have invented him, is she?'

'I –' Nora falters, then catches herself '– no, of course not.'

'Next thing you'll be saying is that she's a bit "that way inclined" too,' Sinead laughs heartily. I hear Juliette try to join in, but it rings false.

'Aha-ha, *really*, Sinead, don't go putting ideas into her head.'

'No, she's right, Juliette, I am being ridiculous.'

'You'll be saying next that she's having an affair with *Miranda*.' The remark falls into a silence. Only Sinead laughs. Jay, I imagine, is panic-stricken, Nora solemn, fighting the hideous notion beginning to take root in her imagination. Suddenly, I hear Sinead's voice, sounding very loud and oddly triumphant, 'Aha, Jay, what's *this*?'

And then Jay's voice, very loud, rendered almost unrecognisable by terror, 'Let me see – oh that, that old thing. That's where it got to. That was just a joke photo a good – straight – friend took of us one day when we were messing about.'

Suddenly things have entered into another dimension. My photo! I shove a few cups and the empty tea-pot onto a tray, and rush back through, in time to hear Jay saying, her voice thick with desperate contempt, '*This* doesn't mean a thing, it's just a waste of a good frame. In fact, I think we should just throw it away –' she turns wildly and sees me standing frozen there '– don't you, Mirry?'

I deliberately drop the tea-tray, hear it crash to the floor. 'Oops – let me see the photo.'

Numbly, she hands it over. I scrutinise it – yes, there we are, lips upturned, gently kissing, smiling into each other's eyes, completely relaxed, completely together. I remember the day it was taken, how happy we were, how joyous I was to have her.

Do I really need any further message to let me know how little it all means to her? I look at Juliette, see nothing but panic and pleading in her eyes now – not pleading for me to forgive her, pleading that her mother will never know.

And I realise, finally, that it's never going to work.

I look back at the photo, and my voice is changed, 'Yes, you're right, it is just a load of old rubbish. What *were* we thinking of, eh?'

And we stare at each other for a highly charged moment, which Nora breaks, her tone harder than I've ever heard it. 'Could I see that photo, please, Jay?'

Jay jumps like a branded filly and rips it from the frame, saying, 'Oh, you don't want to see it, Mam.'

'Sinead, what was that photo of?'

Sinead is still wandering around as if she owned the place. 'Oh, just some stupid photo of Jay and Miranda messing about, pretending to kiss each other or something... just a joke, Mam. Wasn't it it, Jay?'

'Yes,' says Jay, her voice high and strained, 'of course it was. Honestly, Mam... the idea...' and she can't look at me any more.

'You'd better watch it, Jay,' cackles Sinead, a grotesque note of comedy in this black drama of betrayal, 'I really think Mam's got it into her head that you're a lezzie too – aha ha ha. Oh!'

In her incessant quest for... what?... she's pulled open the cupboard that's hiding the strap-on. It now dangles openly from her hand, its black harness and pink shining dildo swinging obscenely in the silence. It's certainly stopped Sinead's merry banter.

'Jay?' she whimpers, looking to her older sister for help, but Juliette's gone a very incriminating scarlet and maybe this is where the lies finally stop.

'Sinead, get your coat.' Nora's voice cuts through the stillness. 'We're leaving.'

'What?'

'Mam?'

'Sinead, I said we're leaving!' Nora's voice is rising to a scarily high pitch.

'But why? I don't even know what that thing's for,' she wails, and I wonder again about her sex life. Surely to God she could hazard a guess?

'... And I don't know when we'll be back. To think we trusted you...' Nora's voice cracks, then regains its harshness. 'There never was a Martin, was there?'

In that breathless hush where Jay looks as if she's about to tell all, I wait so hopefully, thinking that maybe all is not lost. Tell her, Jay, just get the courage to tell her like it's something to be proud of, instead of something to hide in a corner forever. Tell it like it is, and get your self-respect and independence back and lean on me and we will (eventually) live happily – so happily – ever after.

Just as she takes a breath to eventually speak the truth to her mother and I'm poised to catch her, we hear a knock on the outside door and Martin's happy voice calling, 'Ross? Ross, it's Martin...'

'Martin?' says Nora sharply, and '*Martin*!' gasps Jay. '*Martin*!' In a flash, she's up and out the door. I sag in incredulity. Nora is confused, Sinead pleased.

'Oh good! We're finally going to get to meet Martin!' She looks down, sees the dildo still in her hand – 'Eekk!' – and quickly pushes it back into the drawer.

'That *is* Martin, isn't it, Miranda?' Nora asks quietly.

'Why wouldn't it be?' I snarl.

'So you and Juliette aren't...?'

'Oh Mam!' groans Sinead in exasperation, 'She's got... Arabella.' Poor Sinead, forever looking up to her big sister, believing her whatever she says. Are all little sisters like that?

'So I do,' I say.

Nora crumples onto the settee, one hand over her heart. 'Oh, the relief.'

We wait there in complete silence, like some weird Victorian tableau, Sinead by the cupboard, me standing by the door, Nora drooping on the couch, until Jay comes back, tugging a stiff and uneasy Martin behind her.

'Mam... this is Martin.'

Nora gets up like the Queen Mother and moves toward him radiating graciousness. 'I'm very pleased to meet you at last, Martin,' she murmurs, holding out her hand.

'How do you do,' he announces, shaking her hand firmly.

'And Sinead...'

Sinead bounds forward, smiling coyly. 'Hello.'

'Hello,' he beams at her, with a rictus smile. They shake hands too. I'm riveted to the spot.

'So, Martin, sit down.' Nora's still doing her queenly bit.

'Thank you.' He lowers himself carefully into an armchair. 'Hello, Miranda.'

I give him a little wave. 'Hi-i.'

'How was the course?' inquires Nora.

'Oh, it was all right.' Jay certainly briefed him thoroughly.

'But you couldn't wait to get back to Jay here, eh?' grins Sinead.

'That's right,' Martin says woodenly.

'That's so romantic.'

'Ye-e-s...'

'Would anyone like a drink?' Jay asks desperately. 'Sweetheart,' she turns prettily to Martin, 'would you come and help me, please?'

'Sure, pushkin. See, she's got me pretty well trained already.' They vanish into the kitchen, doubtless for another intensive briefing session on what's Gone Before.

Nora looks at Sinead and me. 'Well, he seems very nice.'

'Oh, I think he's gorgeous.'

I sigh, start picking up the spilled cups and saucers. Then there's a cursory knock on the door and Robbie, Ross and Will pile in.

'Hi,' says Robbie breezily, 'hope we're not interrupting anything...'

Nora is looking most discomfited: homosexuals butting in *now*? At this most delicate time!

'But we heard Jay's Martin is back in town, and we couldn't wait to meet him,' Will adds blithely.

'We couldn't not see this,' agrees Ross. Martin re-enters carrying a tray of drinks. Jay has her arm round his waist. '... And here it is. Hi,' he beams, stepping forward, 'I'm Ross.'

Jay takes the tray adroitly away from Martin before he drops it.

'Hello, Ross,' says Martin, glaring daggers at him.

'I'm Robbie.' He steps up in turn, hand outstretched.

'Hello, Robbie.'

'And I'm Will,' smiles the love of Martin's life, stepping skittishly up.

'Pleased to meet you,' says Martin through gritted teeth, giving Will's hand too hearty a shake.

'Likewise.' Will skips back and, much to Martin's discomfort, snuggles up to Ross.

Nora takes her sherry. 'So, Martin, what exactly is it that you do?'

'Well,' he says, darting a haunted glance at Will, who is now casually caressing Ross's neck, 'I'm in computers...'

'Computers,' she nods, 'that's a good job to have, especially these days.'

'Yes, Jay's always telling us about all the things he's buying her,' says Ross, solicitously taking the tray from Juliette. 'I'll take that, dear. You go and snuggle.'

'Lovely,' says Martin lamely, as Jay advances toward him. She sits down clumsily and takes his hand as though it weren't attached to his body. He winces.

'Aaahhh,' Ross, Robbie, Will and Sinead coo in perfect unison.

Ross tinkles, 'That's something you don't see every day.'

'Martin, we were thinking about going out to dinner later... just the four of us,' Nora smiles archly.

Martin, looking as though the nightmare has just deepened infinitely, says, 'Oh... great...'

Ross, Robbie and Will are quietly having hysterics. 'Let's make the most of the love-birds while we've got them, then. Tell us, Jay, how did you two meet? And did you know instantly that he was the man for you?' Robbie asks solicitously.

Jay, aware of Nora and Sinead staring intently at her, snuggles uncomfortably into Martin, who in turn manfully puts his arm round her shoulders and pulls her in tight. It's very awkwardly done, and I know how graceful they can both be.

'Well,' Jay begins, 'we met at a party. And – I don't know – how do you know when it's the right man for you?' She may well ask.

'Oh, you know,' beams Ross, squeezing Will's hand. Will smiles up at him adoringly, which infuriates Martin, who can do nothing about it but attempt revenge by cuddling Jay closer, which in turn makes *me* feel very odd. Oh, this is *fun*.

'So, Martin,' asks Will, with genuine curiosity, 'what does it feel like to have found the right woman?'

'Oh, you know,' fields Martin, 'a bit strange...'

'But wonderfully strange... *darling*,' reminds Jay, with an almost wifely edge in her voice.

'Oh, of course, wonderfully strange. Whoops, nearly in trouble there, eh?'

'Aha-ha, of course not... sweetest.'

They look at each other woodenly.

'Come on, guys,' urges Robbie, 'you're not being very informative here. We want all the goss – what *you* thought when you first saw her, what *you* thought when you first saw him – everything!'

Nora has had enough. 'Well, I'm afraid as it's now nearly –'

she looks at her pearly watch '– nine, and as we were hoping to eat no later than nine-thirty...'

'Say no more,' gasps Robbie, apparently mortified.

'We can take a hint,' Will chimes in, and they all rise, filing past the lovebirds one by one.

'Nice to meet you, Martin,' says Will, shaking his hand again and pecking Jay on the cheek, 'I hope you'll be *very happy* together.' And out he goes.

'Take care of each other,' smiles Robbie. 'Love like this doesn't come along very often. Bye, Mrs and Miss Jay.'

Ross wrings Martin's hand, looks deep into his eyes, 'Have a *fun* evening.'

'I'll see you out,' I say and we all howl silently in the corridor.

When I return, Nora is saying, 'Whew, I thought they'd never leave. Sorry about that, Martin.'

'That's... quite all right...'

She hasn't seen me. 'To tell you the truth, I'll be quite happy when Juliette finally moves out of here.'

'Oh? And why's that?' Martin's voice now has a distinct edge to it. I wouldn't be surprised to hear him add 'pray?' to the end of the sentence, see him draw his sword to defend gay honour.

'Oh, well, you know,' flusters Nora, 'with the neighbours being... the way they are, and –'

'Mam,' Jay interjects, looking nervously at Martin's set white face, 'for God's sake...'

'What, dear? Martin probably agrees with me.'

'Oh, never mind all that. Now that they've gone, tell us all about yourself, Martin,' urges Sinead.

The worst thing about it is how grateful I'd have been if they were saying this to me. It's like being an invisible spectator to meeting them as my in-laws.

'Oh, aha, no,' stutters Martin, horrified at the thought.

'Oh, go on... we've been dying to meet you for ages,' she coaxes, while I, the actual lover of her sister, stand there thinking, 'you should be saying that to me.'

'No, no,' Martin refuses firmly to elaborate on himself. 'So, is Jay going to be moving out of here soon then?'

I look up sharply.

'No I am not. Really, Mam.' She glances at me, then away. 'Sorry, Miranda.'

'Don't let *that* worry you.'

'Miranda,' says Martin, now completely at sea, 'do you have a boyfriend too?'

Sinead sniggers.

'No,' I say quietly, 'actually, I have a girlfriend, Martin.'

'You do?'

'Yes, her name's Arabella,' I say. (Martin, who's been taking a crafty and much-needed swig of sherry, jumps and chokes.) 'And she should actually be here –' there is a timid knock on the door '– right now.' I smile at him, ignoring the sense of creeping unreality that is taking over.

'This *has* turned into a more interesting evening than the one I had planned,' he states.

'Yes, I'm sorry,' says Nora.

I roll my eyes and go to the door. There's no time to fill Arabella in on the events of the evening. All I can do is whisper, 'You're my girlfriend, don't act surprised by anything.'

'After last night?' she mutters back. 'You must be joking.'

By the time we get back in, Martin is saying, his face flushed, 'Well, I'm afraid I'm not homophobic, so –'

On seeing us, and unsure how much Arabella knows, he jumps up immediately to shake hands with her, gabbling, 'Hello Arabella I'm Jay's boyfriend Martin.'

'Hello, Martin,' she says, shaking his hand too vigorously from nerves, 'I'm Miranda's girlfriend, I don't know if they told you...'

Oh, our poor friends. How did we get them into this?

'They did, yes, nice to meet you.'

'You too.' Then they stand there like a couple of amateur actors who've said their lines too quickly and don't know how to fill the space until the rest of the cast come back. In the end Arabella's stiff-upper-lipped cocktail manners come to the rescue, and she smiles at Nora and Sinead and says, 'Hello again,' and the stupid bitches look at her like she's something the cat's dragged in and nod briefly before turning away. This is too blatant to be overlooked.

'I'm sorry, Arabella,' I say, 'I'm afraid that Jay's family are all extremely homophobic... sounds like a disease, doesn't it?'

Nora wades into battle with me at last. 'We're not the ones who're... afflicted, Miranda. If disapproving of a lifestyle that's patently unnatural and against God's law sounds like a disease to you, then well, you certainly are on the wrong path.' She tuts to show her utter disgust with me and it does scrape something against my heart. I was fond of this woman, thought she liked me too. She turns fiercely to Arabella. 'What do your parents think about it?'

'They've been fi–'

'Bloody awful about it, haven't they, darling? She was scared to tell them at first. We had to sneak around for years. It was horrible, and it affected her and our relationship badly...'

'Yes, it did,' Arabella agrees.

I look at Jay. 'But then, in the end, we decided that, if we loved each other as much as we said we did, then there simply wasn't a choice. If we were important enough to each other to love and live together, it was just too ridiculous and demeaning not to tell her parents.'

And I gaze at Jay, my Jay, my Jay whom I've lost, whom I never really had, and wonder if she understands anything at all.

'It was very brave of Arabella to do it and I love her so much for it, for trusting me and "us" enough to take that step into the unknown, to say that this was important enough for her to risk losing her family over. That meant everything to me, made me feel unbelievably loved and valued, instead of cheap, and infinitely expendable.'

Jay looks away.

'And how did her parents take it?' asks Nora.

'Oh, they rejected her at first, were every bit as nasty as she'd feared they'd be.'

'I'm not surprised. It is an unnatural –'

'As unnatural as rejecting your own child for it?' Martin suddenly challenges her, his voice harsh.

Nora is a bit taken aback at this. Jay nudges him in the ribs. 'Darling, you're talking to my mother, *who you're trying to impress.*'

'Some things are unacceptable, Martin,' that mother states sharply. As he opens his mouth to argue, Jay pokes him again. He subsides, wheezing, and glares at her.

'Sorry, *darling.*'

I pick up the ball, run with it. 'Yes, Nora, some things are unacceptable – rudeness, cruelty and lack of love are unacceptable to me, as is unreasoning prejudice and a hopelessly ignorant and judgemental attitude.' As I gain confidence, my voice steadies. 'Things that hurt the innocent are wrong and a lack of understanding for something that is no crime is terribly, terribly wrong. Some parents manage to forgive their children truly evil things – murder, rape, child abuse – but you would reject yours simply for falling in love and being happy!'

I stop. There is silence. I'm foolish enough to think that maybe I've swayed her a little, when she says, 'It's wrong, Miranda, and I think it's high time we left.'

As she moves towards her coat in high dudgeon, Jay's voice stops her, and again my heart lifts.

'Wait a minute, Mam. Arabella, what happened with your parents in the long run?'

'Oh,' she says, her crisp patrician vowels adding extra weight to her words, 'they eventually came round to it a bit and now we see them. It's not perfect, but it's a lot better than it was, and at least I don't feel constantly terrified now and guilty and continually ashamed of myself.'

I look at Jay, surprised yet again to find that I'm crying.

'You see, Mam,' she is saying, 'parents do eventually come to terms with it. As long as your child's happy, what difference does it make if they're happy straight, or happy gay? Even you'd come round to it too, in the end.'

And I sniff and wipe my eyes, because I know that she's never going to tell them, that this is the best she can do and it isn't nearly good enough.

Nora gets up decisively, brushing her daughter's words off her.

'Right, we really are going to have to go now. Sinead, get your coat.'

Sinead gets up with alacrity.

Nora shoves hers on like a warrior, albeit one who's on the wrong side, 'And no, Juliette, neither your father nor I would ever tolerate homosexuality in our family and you should be grateful for that, that you've been brought up properly and –' here she takes a deep, cleansing breath '– let's go and have a proper, *normal* family dinner.' She marches out without a backward glance, her gay daughter and homosexual pretend-son-in-law following.

The front door bangs. Nora's voice, exultant with family values, is borne back to us on the breeze, saying, 'Right, so where shall we go?' and then their footsteps fade away.

Arabella and I sit there in silence.

'Poor Martin,' she says at last.

'Poor Jay,' I mutter and, turning away before I weep, 'That's it, then.'

Sixteen

The night they leave, she sprawls in an armchair and says contentedly, 'Thank goodness we're finally back to normal, eh?'

Back to normal? Did she dream her way through the visit and all its ramifications?

'Yeah,' I say, too exhausted for a show-down.

'Why don't you come and sit beside me?' she asks.

'I'm fine here, thanks.'

'Suit yourself.'

No, I'm going. This isn't my idea of life and love. I'll just have to wait, choose the moment.

In the next two weeks, Jay and I are as polite as strangers, and just as warm. I think she knows something's up, but in her arrogance or her not caring, she doesn't ask – something else I can't forgive.

I take the day off work to pack and I'm flinging things hurriedly into a suitcase when there's a knock on the door. It's Ross. We've been too ashamed to see our friends since that night but he comes in now as though nothing's happened, breezy as ever.

'I won't stay long, pumpkin. I heard you banging around down here and I just popped down to invite you to our Six-Four anniversary party. That's six months married, four years living in sin – next Saturday!'

'Oh, that's really nice –' I will not think about what might have been for Jay and me '– but I won't be able to make it.'

'And why not?' he demands huffily.

I cough to disguise what was going to be either a crazy laugh or a sob. 'I won't be here – living here – any more.'

'Ah.'

It's not a shock.

'Yes. I've finally had enough, and I'm – I'm leaving her.'

'Ahhh.'

'Do you think I've made the wrong decision?'

Ross suddenly comes to life. 'No. God, no, who could blame you?' and I get a glimmer of what it might be like to be treated as a human again.

'Jay?'

'Ah, who knows with Jay? Probably she will, but that's tough... you took it for a good long time.'

'And it was all for nothing.'

Ross sits down beside me, puts his arm round me. I lean into him, but I'm tense, so tense.

'No, no, it wasn't for nothing. Not at all. You tried... and you two had something special... in between all the shouting.'

'Not special to Jay.'

'Jay's an idiot.'

I sniff, half-laugh. 'I know... I loved her...' And then the tears come. Ross lets me cry, holding me. I want to scream against his shirt that it isn't *fair*, this pain, that I'm being suffocated in it, that I can't see a way out of it. That everything is a nightmare now – this room, with its plants and blinds shut against the afternoon light, the thought of tomorrow with no Juliette in it. The thought of the rest of my life, stretching out flat, pointless and unreal as a cartoon, without her.

Eventually, tears take some of this instalment of the pain away. I sit up sniffing, feeling a thin sword in my side, twisting whenever I move. Nauseating. It's the knowledge that Jay will take this as proof of my worthlessness, reinforcing how right she was not to love me. It's the realisation that there's no going back now.

'Sorry.'

'Don't be an idiot.'

We sit for a while in companionable silence. The ache in me dims a little with the peace of it.

'You can still come, you know,' Ross says suddenly.

'What?'

'To the party...'

'What about Jay?'

'Jay can go fuck herself.'

I sob on a laugh and lean against him a bit more.

We sit there until the light fails, until it's time for Jay to come home.

Seventeen

'Good evening,' she says, marching in as usual, flinging her keys possessively onto the table. She's about to stalk into the kitchen for the first Guinness of the evening, when something hits her. She stops, peering accusingly at me.

'You're home early.'

'I didn't go in today.'

'Why not?'

I swallow. Suddenly I'm terrified. 'I had a few things to do here today.'

'Like what?' Either she senses something's not right, or she's scared I've taken control of the flat and *moved things about,* because she swings round like a hound dog that's just caught the trail of a fox. I swallow again.

'I... I was packing.' I look at her, nerve myself to say it. It feels like I'm tearing in two. 'I'm leaving.'

'What?' She looks dazed, her eyes have gone blank. I collapse onto that bloody sofa.

'Come on, Jay, you know it's been crap between us since the whole Martin thing... it's never exactly been smooth sailing, but that just put the tin lid on it.'

Half of me wants this to be over; for her to just say, 'Yes, you're right, I'll leave you to get on.' The other half, rising up in me like a thunderstorm, desperately wants her to cry, 'NO! You can't go – I need you! I've been a fool but I'll change.'

And she gets it nearly right. 'But you can't be leaving, I won't let you.' But she is too dazed to make it sound convincing, still reeling from the shock.

'No,' I snap, 'what you didn't do was let me stay... let me in. You were never in this a hundred per cent, were you, and one hundred per cent from both sides is what it takes to make a relationship work, maybe especially a gay one – I don't know. What I do know,' I quieten down, forlorn, 'is that you don't love me.'

'That's rubbish,' she says angrily, 'that is such *absolute crap*.'

I struggle for the truth, because neither of us have it yet.

'I think you love me a little,' I say slowly, 'I think you love the bit of me that loves you and takes care of you, but that's not loving *me*.'

'But I *do* love you.' She paces forward, runs her hands through her hair in desperate frustration. All my planned speeches have gone out the window, faced with her aura, bashing against mine. I'm on the verge of being taken over again, of relaxing into the warmth.

'I think,' I almost sob, struggling for the words I don't want to have to say, the obvious ones, 'I *think*, if you really loved me, really "in love" loved me, then you'd have been able to tell your parents about this and cope with it if they rejected you. Because I was able to do it for you – there wasn't anyone or anything I wouldn't have sacrificed for you, for this.' I am crying. I wipe a tear away, laugh at the loss: 'I thought that this was the most wonderful, precious thing – something to treasure, and keep safe. I thought that this was our safety; I thought that this was the greatest privilege and joy; that this was what life was all about and there was nothing that I wouldn't have done for it.'

'But I feel that too,' she cries desperately and I wonder at our ability to deceive ourselves, both of us.

'Of course you don't. If you did, you'd have told your parents a long time ago, or, if not then, you certainly wouldn't have let them treat me like they did when they were here. But it was you tearing up that photograph in front of me that finally made me realise that you don't really give a shit about me, not *really*. You'd fling me to the sharks in a second if that was what it took to keep your dirty little secret safe from Mammy and Daddy and... Sinead... and that's not love,' I finish, panting, and pain leaks through me from the thousand places where the dream's been pushed away. I think my heart has just folded up.

'You're talking rubbish.' Her voice is hard.

'No I'm not. You've treated me and this relationship like dirt since it first started, and whether it's because you're ashamed of it, or because you're terrified your parents'll find out, or because you're not truly in love with me, I don't know. I'm just tired of all the pain and now I don't have the hope any longer that, if I just try harder, this time it'll be all right, this time I'll get through to you. I've tried hard enough, been good enough to be really loved by you.'

Anger is fading; desolation comes softly but with destruction in its wake, showing me the barrenness of a landscape I thought was crowded with joy. I take a desperate look back, before the colours fade altogether, see Jay as I used to, surrounded by scarlets and blacks, silver and gold and the deep blue the evening sky was the May that I fell in love with her. 'I love you *so much*, you know...'

'And I love you...' Tears are streaming down her face. Impatiently she wipes them away. Her voice is choked. 'Look, I'm not letting you go. Stay here tonight, *yes*, you're staying, and we'll talk and I *will* tell my parents, I will...'

'All right then – phone them up now and tell them and I'll stay forever. Go on. Right now, you pick up that phone and you tell them that you're in love with a woman, and that it's the joy of your life, so joyous and lovely, in fact, that if you never hear from them again you won't mind, because you'll have this.' She is mute. 'Well? Are you going to?'

Silence. Then Juliette stirs wearily, sighs as though she's

carrying the weight of the world and says, 'You know I can't.'

'No I don't... not any more. Thousands of gay people do it every day, because that's how much they love their partners. You always made me think that it was such a big deal, Juliette, but it's not. It's not. Not if you love me.' I take a ragged breath. There. I've said it and the pain of realisation setting in almost undoes me.

'It's not like that.' She is at bay now, twisting and turning. 'You don't have a good relationship with your parents. How would you know what it's like?'

Anger flashes through me. 'I've got a better relationship with mine than you'll ever have with yours – it's honest, and I know they'd never turn me away, whatever I'd done.'

Thinking about our respective parents stuns us into silence, while the weight of them hangs heavy in the air.

'Please stay,' she begs, eventually.

I am still bitterly angry. 'What, for more of the same? I don't think so.'

'We've had some good times. You're talking as if it's been nothing but heartache,' she says, her throat closing on the words, pain radiating off her.

'Yes, we have and after every lovely time, you'd find some way of freezing me out, and it *hurt*, Juliette, because I let all my defences down, I let you in completely. I always had to be so good, never take it for granted, always be "there", while you – you could just be yourself and, if I didn't like it, then tough, I was on my own. That's not a relationship. That's like being a sort of emotional servant.' I pause. 'You're never going to get over the fact that you're gay, are you? Or maybe it's just that you're not in love with me...' I wait for her denial, which doesn't come and, amazingly, that still hurts me. The barriers are down now – we're laid open for the utter truth.

'I don't know... neither. I *am* in love with you. Just give me another chance, and I'll prove it.'

It's getting dark outside. I am stiff and chilled; soon I'll have to go. We're down to the bare bones now. There's nothing left.

'I did give you another chance... Phone your parents, I said. Do you remember that?'

'You know I can't do that,' she replies inevitably.

'And I can't stay here if you don't. It's been too much pain, Jay, for too little reward.' I remember the Siberia analogy. 'Sunbathing in Siberia. Dark and cold where there should be warmth and light.' I gasp, remembering what it was like.

'But you could say that about all gay relationships... we're all bloody "sunbathing in Siberia",' she protests, 'until society changes.'

'Society *has* changed,' I snap, 'only people like you and your family don't realise it yet. The thaw's set in. We could have been *happy*...'

The sentence seems to reverberate, filling the room with images of what might have been.

'I'm sorry,' she says simply.

'Don't be... you're not losing anything you really want to keep.'

'That is just not *true,*' she cries on a note of pure pain, and the tears well up again, choking her. She struggles against it, then gives in and cries, bowing her face onto the arm of her chair. I sigh, wonder for the thousandth time why she chooses this pain, how she can feel this pain and not fix it.

I stand up stiffly, walk over to her, look down at her for a moment as she weeps. Desolation is almost palpable, like an aura around her. I touch the dark head lightly and, even as I wonder how I can bear to, I am walking away.

Epilogue

Two years passed and I didn't meet anyone who even came close to her. Indeed, meeting others only served to remind me of how perfect it had been, at its best, with Jay.

The last time I heard of her, she'd gone home to Ireland, where Owen and Sinead were trying to find her a husband. The mind boggles.

Apparently, when I left, she told her mother it was because I'd broken up with Arabella and needed a change.

'Well, those sort of relationships never seem to last, do they?' Nora sneered. 'I don't know why...'

I only hope Jay caught the irony of it all.

I wonder if she thinks of me, now she's safe in her homeland. I wonder if she remembers.

Ross and Robbie are still happily married. The bash they threw for their 24/8 Anniversary was the talk of the entire Gay Community.

Arabella and Pamela have had a baby boy, called Rupert in an attempt to woo the baby's crusty old grandfather. I think it worked; when last seen, Baby Rupert was being pushed in his impeccable Silver Cross pram by Sir Rupert, who was muttering earnestly to him about the importance of liking *girls*. As if it was hereditary.

Martin continues to be led a merry dance by Will and, so far at least, is thriving on it.

And me? I needed to get out of London for a bit, so I got a transfer to Brighton and a flat there. But I love London, and I'll go back one day.

In darker moments – and there have been very dark moments – I have wondered, is it all my fault? Am I too unforgiving? Is it *not* that they are too cold for me, all of them, but that I demand too much? Am I just set at the wrong temperature for love? Was I not strong enough to cope with the inevitable cracks in it?

Juliette and I had each longed for a magical place that shone with the approval and affection of our parents. The difference between us was that she was already in hers, but it rocked and shifted whenever the winds of homophobia blew. I, on the other hand, was always seeking it: that magical place which I never reached with Bill, that green shining corner which could not be permanent, but which, with Jay, I could live in for a while.

For me, though, that magic land has to be guarded by the

twin dragons of contempt and dislike, or it's not the right place. No wonder I loved Jay. No wonder people who have lousy parents go for the same again. That enchanted place of love and acceptance and belonging could be laid out in front of us, but if the dragons weren't there at the gate, we wouldn't recognise it. We need to see those dragons – and we're always hoping that, this time, we'll be able to slay them.

They say there's a love map imprinted on us before we're five which is made up of our parents' characteristics. And when we meet someone who fits that map, that's when we fall in love.

But I don't know. When I fell in love with Jay, I thought she was marvellous; I fell in love with her freshness and her generosity, and it took me a long time to realise how like Bill she could be. I loved her in spite of the similarities, not because of them. We had something special and when she let it be, it was perfect. And after I left, I still kept waiting for the happy ending, expecting her to realise what a mistake she'd made and come and find me...

Then I met Serena and everything changed again. Adaptability. That's the key.

New from Diva Books

Treasure

Helen Larder

The hunt is on!

It's Jo's birthday and her girlfriend Sarah has organised a treasure hunt in the country for the two of them, their little girl Derrie and their friends.

But each woman has a different quest: while Sarah needs to know if Jo is planning to leave her, Andi is pursuing Somoya, Somoya is running from her own demons and Charlotte is struggling to fit in. They only take their eyes off Derrie for a moment, but it's a moment too long.

With fast cars, feverish lust and magical visions, *Treasure* is an enchanting summer ride and a celebration of love and friendship.

"Helen Larder's debut novel is a gentle comedy of manners that contains more than a few twists and turns, red herrings and literary sleights of hand... It's a witty, thoughtful and well-written foray into domestic lesbian life that many of its readers will recognise. Larder builds up tension nicely" ★★★

Rainbow Network

RRP £8.99 ISBN 1-873741-81-2

The Woman in Beige
V.G. Lee

A brilliant offbeat comedy

Lorna has a paper round and her dole cheques to support her in her mission to complete The Alternative Alternative Cookbook. The only distractions are Mr E in his wilderness garden with the giant albino rabbit Alfred the Great and a woman called Dan who dresses in beige and makes Lorna's heart leap with every encounter. But it won't be long before Dan's strange behaviour makes Lorna suspect her of a most peculiar crime...

"A strange mix of noir, romance and a London that seems more like *Twin Peaks* **than** *This Life*. **Recommended even for those who don't like beige"** ★★★★ *What's On UK*

"An accomplished novelist" *Gay City News*

"An entertaining read" *Big Issue*

"Always entertaining and often incisive, especially when dealing firmly with bitter-sweet basic human frailties and counsellors in paisley pantaloon outfits" *Time Out*

"In the same vein as Alan Bennett and Victoria Wood, albeit somewhat darker in tone" ★★★ *Rainbow Network*

"Seriously funny... V.G. Lee's talent is that she writes about the little things in life like nobody else" *G3*

RRP £8.99 ISBN 1-873741-80-4

Groundswell

The Diva Book of Short Stories 2

Edited by Helen Sandler

The follow-up to the acclaimed Lambda-winning Diva Book of Short Stories

With stories from Ali Smith, Emma Donoghue and Jackie Kay plus two dozen more writers from the UK and North America, every reader will want to join this groundswell.

"Plenty of good stuff" *Guardian*

"Helen Sandler has outdone herself with a wonderful mix of short stories by British, American and Canadian lesbian authors" *Gay City News*

"Sandler has excelled herself" ★★★★★ *The List*

"From lightweight to luscious and all things in between... an Everywoman of lesbian writing" ★★★★ *Big Issue*

"An impressive castlist" *Time Out*

"The breadth of material is stunning" *Our World*

"Proof that new lesbian fiction is alive and kicking... A real accomplishment" ★★★★ *Rainbow Network*

"Something for everyone" ★★★★★ *Out in Greater Manchester*

RRP £9.99 ISBN 1-873741-77-4